DON'T POINT THAT THING AT ME

KYRIL BONFIGLIOLI

THE OVERLOOK PRESS
Woodstock & New York

This paperback edition first published in the United States in 2004 by
The Overlook Press, Peter Mayer Publishers, Inc.
Woodstock & New York

WOODSTOCK:
One Overlook Drive
Woodstock, NY 12498
www.overlookpress.com
[for individual orders, bulk and special sales, contact our Woodstock office]

NEW YORK:
141 Wooster Street
New York, NY 10012

Cataloging-in-Publication Data is available from the Library of Congress

Book design and type formatting by Bernard Schleifer
Printed in the United States of America
ISBN 1-58567-562-8
3 4 5 6 7 8 9 10

DON'T POINT THAT THING AT ME

The epigraphs are all by Robert Browning, except one, which is a palpable forgery.

This is not an autobiographical novel: it is about some *other* portly, dissolute, immoral and middle-aged art dealer. The rest of the characters are quite imaginary too, especially that Mrs. Spon, but most of the places are real.

1

So old a story, and tell it no better?
Pippa Passes

When you burn an old carved and gilt picture frame it makes a muted hissing noise in the grate – a sort of genteel *fooh* – and the gold leaf tints the flames a wonderful peacock blue-green. I was watching this effect smugly on Wednesday evening when Martland came to see me. He rang the bell three times very fast, an imperious man in a hurry. I was more or less expecting him, so when my thug Jock put his head around the door, eyebrows elaborately raised, I was able to put a certain aplomb into my 'Wheel him in.'

Somewhere in the trash he reads Martland has read that heavy men walk with surprising lightness and grace; as a result he trips about like a portly elf hoping to be picked up by a leprechaun. In he pranced, all silent and catlike and absurd, buttocks swaying noiselessly.

'Don't get up,' he sneered, when he saw that I had no intention of doing so. 'I'll help myself, shall I?'

Ignoring the more inviting bottles on the drinks tray, he unerringly snared the great Rodney decanter from underneath and poured himself a gross amount of what he thought would be my Taylor '31. A score to me already, for I had filled it with Invalid Port of an unbelievable nastiness. He didn't notice: score two to me. Of course, he is only a policeman. Perhaps 'was' by now.

He lowered his massive bum into my little *Régence fauteuil* and smacked his lips courteously over the crimson garbage in his glass. I could almost hear him scrabbling about in his brain for a deft, light opening. His Oscar Wilde touch. Martland has only two personalities – Wilde and Eeyore. Nevertheless, he is a very cruel and dangerous policeman. Or perhaps 'was' – or have I said that?

'My dear boy,' he said finally, 'such ostentation. Even your fire-wood is gilded now.'

'An old frame,' I said, playing it straight. 'Thought I'd burn it.'

'But such a waste. A nice Louis Seize carved frame . . .'

'You know bloody well it isn't a nice Louis anything frame,' I snarled. 'It's a repro Chippendale trailing-vine pattern made about last week by one of those firms in the Greyhound Road. Came off a picture I bought the other day.'

You never know what Martland knows or doesn't know, but I felt fairly safe on the subject of antique frames: even Martland couldn't have taken a course on them, I thought.

'Would have been interesting if it had been a Louis Seize one though, you must admit; say about 50 by 110 centimetres,' he mumbled, gazing meditatively at the last of it glowing in the grate.

At that point my thug came in and deposited about twenty pounds of coal onto it and retired after giving Martland a civil smile. Jock's idea of a civil smile is rolling back part of his upper lip from a long, yellow dogtooth. It frightens age.

'Listen, Martland,' I said evenly. 'If I had lifted that Goya, or fenced it, you can't really think that I'd bring it here in its frame, for God's sake? And then burn the frame in my own grate? I mean, I'm not a *dullard*, am I?'

He made embarrassed, protesting noises as though nothing was further from his thoughts than the princely Goya whose theft from Madrid had filled the newspapers for the past five days. He helped out the noises by flapping his hands a bit, slopping some of the alleged wine onto a nearby rug.

'That,' I said crisply, 'is a valuable Savonnerie rug. Port is bad for it. Moreover, there is probably a priceless Old Master cunningly concealed beneath it. Port would be very bad for that.'

He leered at me nastily, knowing that I was quite possibly telling the truth. I leered back coyly, knowing that I was telling the truth.

From the shadows beyond the doorway my thug Jock was smiling his civilest smile. We were all happy to the casual eye, had there been such an eye on the premises.

At this stage, before anyone starts to think that Martland is, or was, an ineffectual neddy, I had better fill in a bit of background. You doubtless know that, except under very extraordinary circumstances, English policemen never carry any weapon but the old Punch-and-Judy wooden truncheon. You know too that they never, never resort to physical unkindness – they dare not even spank the bottoms of little boys caught scrumping apples nowadays, for fear of assault charges and official inquiries and Amnesty International.

You know all this for certain, because you have never heard of the Special Powers Group – SPG – which is a peculiar kind of outsider-police squad conjured up by the Home Office during a fit of fact-facing in the weeks following the Great Train Robbery. The SPG was engendered by an Order in Council and has something called a Sealed Mandate from the Home Secretary and one of his more permanent civil servants. It is said to cover five sheets of brief-paper and has to be signed afresh every three months. The burden of its song is that only the nicest and most balanced chaps are to be recruited into the SPG, but that, once in, they are to be allowed to get away with murder – to say the least – so long as they get results. There are to be no more Great Train jobs, even if this entails – perish the thought – bashing a few baddies without first standing them expensive trials. (It's saved a fortune in dock-briefs already.) All the newspapers, even the Australian-owned sort, have made a deal with the Home Office whereby they get the stories hot from the septic tank in exchange for sieving out the firearms-and-torture bit. Charming.

The SPG – or SOGPU as I've heard it called – needs have no further truck with the Civil Service except for one horrified little man in the Treasury; and its Mandate instructs – if you please *instructs* – Commissioners of Police to afford them 'all administrative facilities without disciplinary obligations or clerical formalities'. The regular police love that bit, naturally. The SPG is answerable only to the Queen's First Minister through its Procurator, who is a belted Earl and a Privy Councillor and hangs about public lavatories late at night.

Its actual, executive head is a former colonel of paratroops who was at school with me and has the curious rank of Extra Chief Superintendent. Very able chap, name of Martland. Likes hurting people, a lot.

He would dearly have liked to hurt me a bit there and then, in an inquiring sort of way, but Jock was hovering outside the door, belching demurely now and then to remind me that he was on call if required. Jock is a sort of anti-Jeeves: silent, resourceful, respectful even, when the mood takes him, but sort of drunk all the time, really, and fond of smashing people's faces in. You can't run a fine-arts business these days without a thug and Jock is one of the best in the trade. Well, you know, was.

Having introduced Jock – his surname escapes me, I should think it would be his mother's – I suppose I had better give a few facts about myself. I am Charlie Mortdecai. I mean, I was actually christened Charlie; I think my mother was perhaps getting at my father in some obscure way. The Mortdecai tag I am very happy with: a touch of ancientry, a hint of Jewry, a whiff of corruption – no collector can resist crossing swords with a dealer called Mortdecai, for God's sake. I am in the prime of life, if that tells you anything, of barely average height, of sadly over-average weight and am possessed of the intriguing remains of rather flashy good looks. (Sometimes, in a subdued light, and with my tummy tucked in, I could almost fancy me myself.) I like art and money and dirty jokes and drink. I am very successful. I discovered at my goodish second-rate Public School that almost anyone can win a fight if he is prepared to put his thumb into the other fellow's eye. Most people cannot bring themselves to do it, did you know that?

Moreover, I'm a Hon., for my daddy was Bernard, First Baron Mortdecai of Silverdale in the County Palatine of Lancaster. He was the second greatest art dealer of the century: he poisoned his life trying to overprice Duveen out of the field. He got his barony ostensibly for giving the nation a third of a million pounds' worth of good but unsaleable art, but actually for forgetting something embarrassing he knew about someone. His memoirs are to be published after my brother's death, say about next April, with any luck. I recommend them.

Meanwhile, back at the Mortdecai bunkhouse, old straw boss Martland was fretting, or pretending to. He is a terrible actor, but then he is pretty terrible when he's not acting, so it's often difficult to tell, if you follow me.

'Oh, come on, Charlie,' he said petulantly. I gave just enough flicker of the eyebrow to indicate that we had not been at school together all that recently.

'How do you mean, "Come on"?' I asked.

'I mean, let's stop playing silly buggers.'

I considered three clever retorts to that one but found that I couldn't really be bothered. There are times when I am prepared to bandy words with Martland, but this was one of the other times.

'Just what,' I asked reasonably, 'do you think I might give you that you think you might want?'

'Any sort of a lead on the Goya job,' he said in his defeated Eeyore voice. I raised an icy eyebrow or two. He squirmed a bit.

'There are diplomatic considerations, you know,' he moaned faintly.

'Yes,' I said with some satisfaction, 'I see how there might be.'

'Just a name or an address, Charlie. Or anything, really. You must have heard something.'

'And where would the old *cui bono* enter in?' I asked. 'Where is the well-known carrot? Or are you leaning on the old school spirit again?'

'It could buy you a lot of peace and quiet, Charlie. Unless, of course, you happened to be in the Goya trade yourself, as a principal.'

I pondered ostentatiously awhile, careful not to seem too eager, thoughtfully guzzling the real Taylor '31 which was inhabiting my glass.

'All right,' I said at last. 'Middle-aged, rough-spoken chap in the National Gallery, name of Jim Turner.'

The Martland ballpoint skittered happily over the regulation notebook.

'Full name?' he asked briskly.

'James Mallord William.'

He started to write it down, then froze, glaring at me evilly.

'1775 to 1851,' I quipped. 'Stole from Goya all the time. But then old Goya was a bit of a tea leaf himself, wasn't he?'

I have never been so near to getting a knuckle-sandwich in my life. Luckily for what's left of my patrician profile, Jock aptly entered, bearing the television set before him like an unabashed unmarried mum. Martland let prudence rule.

'Har har,' he said politely, putting the notebook away.

'Tonight is Wednesday, you see,' I explained.

'?'

'Professional wrestling. On the telly. Jock and I never miss it; so many of his friends play. Won't you stay and watch?'

'Good night,' said Martland.

For nearly an hour Jock and I regaled ourselves – and the SPG tape recorders – with the grunts and brays of the catchweight kings and the astonishingly lucid commentary of Mr Kent Walton, the only man I can think of who is wholly good at his job.

'That man is astonishingly lucid, etc.,' I said to Jock.

'Yeah. For a minute back there I thought he'd have had the other bugger's ear off.'

'No, Jock, not Pallo. Kent Walton.'

'Well, it looks like Pallo to me.'

'Never mind, Jock.'

'O.K., Mr Charlie.'

It was a splendid programme: all the baddies cheated shamefully, the referee never quite caught them at it, but the good guys always won by a folding press at the last minute. Except in the Pallo bout, naturally. So satisfactory. It was satisfactory, too, to think of all the clever young career bobbies who would, even then, be checking every Turner in the National Gallery. There are a great many Turners in the National Gallery. Martland was smart enough to know that I wouldn't have made a feeble joke just to tease him: every Turner would be checked. Tucked behind one of them, no doubt, his men would find an envelope. Inside – again, no doubt – would be one of those photographs.

When the last bout had ended – with a dramatic Boston Crab this time – Jock and I drank some whisky together, as is our custom on wrestling nights. Red Hackle de Luxe for me and Johnny Walker for

Jock. He prefers it; also, he knows his station in life. We had by then, of course, unstuck the little microphone that Martland had carelessly left behind under the seat of the *fauteuil*. (Jock had been sitting there, so the recorder had doubtless picked up rude noises as well as the wrestling.) Jock, with rare imagination, dropped the little bug into a tumbler, adding water and an Alka-Seltzer tablet. Then he got the giggles, a horrid sight and sound.

'Calm yourself, Jock,' I said, 'for there is work to be done. *Que hodie non est, eras erit*, which means that tomorrow, at about noon, I expect to be arrested. This must take place in the Park if possible, so that I can make a scene if I think fit. Immediately afterwards this flat will be searched. You must not be here, nor must you-know-what. Put it in the headcloth of the hardtop as before, put the hardtop on the MGB and take it to Spinoza's for service. Make sure that you see Mr Spinoza himself. Be there at eight sharp. Got that?'

'Yes, Mr Charlie.'

With that he toddled off to his bedroom down the hall, where I could hear him still giggling and farting happily. His bedroom is neat, simply furnished, full of fresh air: just what you would wish your Rover Scout son's room to be. On the wall hangs a chart of the Badges and Ranks of the British Army; on the bedside table is a framed photograph of Shirley Temple; on the chest of drawers stands a model galleon, not quite finished, and a tidy pile of *Motor Cycle* magazines. I think he used to use pine disinfectant as an after-shave lotion.

My own bedroom is a pretty faithful reconstruction of the business premises of an expensive whore of the Directoire period. For me it is full of charming memories but it would probably make you – manly British reader – vomit. But there.

I sank into a happy, dream-free sleep, for there is nothing like your catchweight wrestling for purging the mind with pity and terror; it is the only mental catharsis worth the name. Nor is there any sleep so sweet as that of the unjust.

That was Wednesday night and nobody woke me up.

2

I am the man you see here plain enough:
Grant I'm a beast, why, beasts must lead beasts' lives!
Suppose I own at once to tail and claws;
The tailless man exceeds me: but being tailed
I'll lash out lion-fashion, and leave apes
To dock their stump and dress their haunches up,
My business is not to remake myself,
But make the absolute best of what God made. . . .

And as this cabin gets upholstery,
That hutch should rustle with sufficient straw.
                                    Bishop Blougram's Apology

Nobody woke me up until ten o'clock of a beautiful summer's morning, when Jock came in with my tea and the canary, which was
singing its little heart out, as ever. I bade them both good morning:
Jock *prefers* me to greet the canary and it costs nothing to accommo-
date him in so small a matter.

'Ah' I added, 'the good old soothing Oolong or Lapsang!'

'Eh?'

'Bring me my whangee, my yellowest shoes, and the old green
Homburg,' I quoted on. 'I am going into the Park to do pastoral dances'

'Eh?'

'Oh, never mind, Jock. Bertram Wooster speaking, not I.'

'O.K., Mr Charlie.'

I often think that Jock should take up squash. He'd have made a
splendid wall.

'Did you take the MGB in, Jock?'

'Yeah.'

'Good. Everything O.K.?' A silly question, of course, and of
course I paid for it.

'Yeah. Well, uh, the you-know-what was a bit too big to go under the headcloth so I had to cut a bit off the edge, you know.'

'You cut a you what you didn't Jock . . .'

'All right Mr Charlie, just having my joke.'

'Yes, all right Jock. Jolly good. Did Mr Spinoza say anything?'

'Yeah, he said a dirty word.'

'Yes, he would, I suppose.'

'Yeah.'

I embarked on the quotidian *schrecklichkeit* of getting up. With occasional help from Jock I weaned myself gingerly from shower to razor, from dexedrine to intolerable decision about necktie; arriving safely, forty minutes later, at the bourne of breakfast, the only breakfast worth the name, the *cheminot*'s breakfast, the great bowl of coffee laced and gadrooned and filigreed with rum. I was up. I had not been sick. The snail was on the thorn, to name but one.

'I don't think we've *got* a green Homburg, Mr Charlie.'

'It's all right, Jock.'

'I could send the porter's little girl over to Lock's if you like?'

'No, it's all right, Jock.'

'She'd go for half a crown.'

'No, it's all *right*, Jock.'

'O.K., Mr Charlie.'

'You must be out of the flat in ten minutes, Jock. No guns or anything like that left here, of course. All alarms turned on and interlocked. Foto-Rekorda loaded with film and cocked – you know.'

'Yeah, I know.'

'Yeah,' I said, draping an extra set of inverted commas around the word, like the verbal snob I am.

Picture, then, this portly lecher swishing down Upper Brook Street, W.1, all sails set for St. James's Park and high adventure. A tiny muscle twitching in the cheek – perhaps in the best tradition – but otherwise outwardly urbane, poised, ready to buy a bunch of violets from the first drab and toss her a golden sov.; Captain Hugh Drummond-Mortdecai MC, with a music-hall song on his whistling lips and a fold of silk underpants trapped between his well-powdered buttocks, bless him.

They were after me from the moment I emerged, of course – well, not actually *after* me because it was a 'front tail' and very prettily done too: the SPG boys have a year's training, for God's sake – but they didn't pick me up at noon as predicted. Back and forth I went past the pond (saying unforgivable things to my friend the pelican) but all they did was pretend to examine the insides of their absurd hats (bursting with two-way radios, no doubt) and make furtive signals to each other with their red, knobbly hands. I was really beginning to think that I had overrated Martland and was just about to beat up to the Reform Club and make someone give me luncheon – their cold table is the best in the world you know – when:

There they were. One on each side of me. Enormous, righteous, capable, deadly, stupid, unscrupulous, grave, watchful, hating me gently.

One of them laid a restraining hand on my wrist.

'Be off with you,' I quavered. 'Where do you think you are – *Hyde* Park?'

'Mr Mortdecai?' he grumbled capably.

'Stop grumbling capably at me,' I protested, 'this is, as you well know, I.'

'Then I must ask you to come along with me, Sir.'

I gazed at the man. I had no idea that people still said that. Is 'dumbfounded' the word I want?

'Eh?' I said, quoting freely from Jock.

'You must come along o'me, Sir.' He was working well now, really settling in to the put.

'Where are you taking me?'

'Where would you like to go, Sir?'

'Well, er . . . *home*?'

'I'm afraid that wouldn't do, Sir. We wouldn't have our equipmeat there, you see.'

'Equipment? Oh, yes. I quite see. Goodness.' I counted my pulse, my corpuscles and a few other necessary parts. *Equipment*. Dammit, Martland and I had been at school together. They were trying to frighten me, clearly.

'You are trying to frighten me, clearly,' I said.

'No, Sir. Not yet we aren't, Sir.'

Can you think of a really smart answer to that one? Neither could I.

'Oh well then. Off to Scotland Yard, I suppose?' I said brightly, not really hoping much.

'No, really, Sir, that wouldn't do, you know that. They're dead narrow-minded there. We thought perhaps our Cottage Hospital, out Esher way.'

Martland had once, in an expansive moment, told me about the 'Cottage Hospital' – it had given me horrid dreams for days afterward.

'No no no no, no no no,' I cried jovially, 'I couldn't dream of taking you lads so far out of your way.'

'Well then,' said Plug Ugly II, giving tongue for the first time, 'what about your little place in the country, down by Stoke Poges?'

I must admit that here I may have blenched a trifle. My private life is an open book for all to read but I did think that 'Possets' was a retreat known only to a few intimate friends. There was nothing that you could call illegal there but I do have a few bits of equipment myself which other folk might think a bit frivolous. A bit Mr Norris – you know.

'Country cottage?' I riposted, quick as a flash. 'Countrycottage countrycottage countrycottage?'

'Yes, Sir,' said Plug Ugly II.

'Nice and private,' quipped his straight man.

After a few false starts I suggested (unruffled now, suave, cool) what would be nicest of all would be to go and call on old Martland; delightful chap, was at school with me. They seemed happy to fall in with any suggestion I made so long as it was that one, and next thing all three of us were bundling into a chance cruising taxi and P.U.II was mumbling an address into the cabby's ear, as though I didn't know Martland's address as well as my own tax code.

'Northampton Park, *Canonbury?*' I tittered, 'since when has old Martland been calling it Canonbury?'

They both smiled at me, kindly. It was almost as bad as Jock's civil smile. My body temperature dropped quite two degrees, I could feel it. Fahrenheit of course: I have no wish to exaggerate.

'I mean, it's hardly even Islington,' I babbled on, *diminuendo*, 'more Newington Green if you ask me; I mean, what a ridiculous...'

I had just noticed that the interior of the chance cruising taxi was short of a few of the usual fitments, like notices about fares, advertisements, *door handles*. What it did have was a radio-telephone and a single handcuff attached to a ring-bolt in the floor. I sort of fell silent.

They didn't seem to think they needed the handcuff; they sat and looked at me thoughtfully, almost kindly, as though they were aunts wondering what I would like for tea.

We drew up in front of Martland's house just as his basket-work Mini trundled in from the Balls Pond Road end. It parked itself rather badly and disgorged Martland, cross and drenched.

This was both good and bad.

Good, because it meant that Martland couldn't have stayed very long at the siege of my flat: Jock had evidently interlocked all the alarms as instructed and Martland, as he masterfully celluloided his way through my front door, would have been met by a Bull-O-Bashan Mk IV siren and a mightly deluge from the automatic fire sprinklers. Moreover, a piercingly strident bell, inaccessibly high on the street-front wall, would have joined in the fun and lights would have flashed in Half Moon Street Police Station and in the Bruton Street depot of an internationally known security organization which I always call Set-a-Thief. A dinky little Japanese frame-a-second robot camera would have been snapping away from its eyrie in the chandelier and, worst of all, the termagant *concierge* would have come raging up the stairs, her malignant tongue cracking like a Boer's stock whip.

Long before I made friends with Mr Spinoza he had asked some of his friends to 'do my pad' as they say, so I knew the general form. The noise of bells and sirens indescribable, the water ineluctable, the conflict of burly Z-car chaps, hairy-assed Security chaps and ordinary villains quite dreadful and, riding clear and hideous over all, the intolerable scourging of the *concierge's* tongue, not to be borne. Poor Martland, I thought happily.

Perhaps I should explain that –

(a) The SPG people obviously carry no identification and take care

not to be known to the ordinary police, for some of their work con-
sists in sorting out naughty coppers

(b) Certain rats of the underworld have recently, with singular
providence, done some deliberately clumsy and nasty 'jobs' while
posing as SPG

(c) The ordinary police are not particularly keen even on *real* SPG
men and

(d) The mindless bullies in my Security firm always release their
pepper guns, two-way radios, aniline dye sprays, Dobermann Pinscher
dogs and rubber coshes long before they ask any questions.

Goodness, what a mess it must have been. And thanks to the little
camera I would certainly get the whole flat handsomely redecorated
by Mrs. Spon – long overdue, I must say – at someone else's expense.

Goodness, too, how cross Martland must be.

Yes, that was the bad bit, of course. He snapped me one pale glare
as he bounded noiselessly (fat men move with surprising grace etc.)
up the steps, dropped his keys, dropped his hat, stood on it, and finally
preceded us into the house. No good for C. Mortdecai was what I
reckoned all that boded. Plug Ugly II, as he stood aside to let me pass,
looked at me so kindly that I felt my breakfast frothing in the small
intestine. Clenching my buttocks bravely I sauntered in and with a
tolerant snigger surveyed what he probably called The Lounge. I had
not seen curtains of that pattern since I seduced the House Mother in
my Approved School; the carpet was a refugee from a provincial cinema foyer and the wallpaper had little silver-grey flock *fleurs-de-lis*.
Yes, truly. All spotlessly clean, of course. You could have eaten your
dinner off them, if you kept your eyes dosed.

They said I could sit down, in fact they urged me to. I could feel
my liver, heavy and sullen, crowding my heart. I no longer wanted
any luncheon.

Martland, reappearing reclothed, dry, was quite himself again and
full of fun.

'Well well well,' he cried, rubbing his hands, 'well, well.'

'I must be off now,' I said firmly.

'No no no,' he cried, 'why, you've only just come. What would
you like to drink?'

'Same whisky, please.'

'Jolly good.' He poured himself a big one but me none. 'Har, har,' I thought.

'Har, har,' I said, out loud, brave.

'Ho, ho,' he riposted archly.

We sat in silence then for quite five minutes, they obviously waiting for me to start to babble protestingly, me determined to do nothing of the kind, but just worrying a little about making Martland any crosser. The minutes wagged on. I could hear a large, cheap watch ticking in the waistcoat of one of the Plug Uglies, that's how old-fashioned they were. A little immigrant child ran past on the pavement outside shrieking 'M'Gawa! M'Gawa!' or words to that effect. Martland's face had relaxed into the complacent smirk of the master of a lordly house, surrounded by friends and loved ones, sated with port and good talk. The hot, itchy, distant-traffic-buzzing silence fretted on. I wanted to go to the lavatory. They kept on looking at me, politely, attentively. Capably.

Martland at last lumbered to his feet with surprising grace etc. and put a record on the turntable, fastidiously balancing the output to the big Quad stereo speakers. It was that lovely record of trains going by, the one we all bought when we could first afford stereo. I never tire of it.

'Maurice,' he said politely to one of his hooligans, 'would you kindly fetch the twelve-volt high-tension motor-car battery from the charging bench in the basement?

'And Alan,' he went on, 'would you please draw the curtains and take Mr Mortdecai's trousers down?'

Now just what can one do when this sort of thing happens? Struggle? What expression can one wear on the well-bred face? Contempt? Outrage? Dignified unconcern? While I was selecting an expression I was deftly divested of the small clothes and all I registered was funky panic. Martland tactfully turned his back and busied himself coaxing a few more decibels out of the stereo equipment. Maurice – I shall always think of him as Maurice – had tucked the first terminal cosily into place half a minute before Martland signalled lewdly for the second to be clipped on. Beautifully timed, the

Flying Scotsman whooped stereophonically for a level crossing. I competed in mono.

And so the long day wore on. Not for many minutes, I must admit. I can stand anything but pain; moreover, the thought that someone is deliberately hurting me, and not minding, upsets me badly. They seemed to know instinctively the point at which I had decided to cry *capivi* for when I came round after that time they had put my trousers back on and there was a great glass of whisky three inches from my nose, with beaded bubbles winking at the brim. I drank it while their faces swam swooningly into focus; they looked kind, pleased with me, proud of me. I was a credit to them, I felt.

'Are you all right, Charlie?' asked Martland, anxiously.

'I must go to the lavatory now,' I said.

'So you shall, dear boy, so you shall. Maurice, help Mr M.'

Maurice took me down to the children's loo; they wouldn't be back from school for another hour, he told me. I found the Margaret Tarrant squirrels and bunnies soothing. I needed soothing.

When we got back to the Lounge the gramophone was dispensing Swan Lake, if you please. Martland has a very simple mind: he probably puts Ravel's Bolero on the turntable when seducing shopgirls.

'Tell me all about it,' he said gently, almost caressingly, his impression of a Harley Street abortionist.

'My bottom hurts,' I whined.

'Yes, yes,' he said. 'But the photograph.'

'Ah,' I said sagely, wagging my head, 'the phokodarts. You have given me too much whisky on an umpty stemach. You *know* I haven't had any lunch.' And with that I gave them some of the whisky back rather dramatically. Martland looked vexed but I thought the effect on his sofa cover was something of an improvement. We got through the next two or three minutes without too much damaging the new-found amenities. Martland explained that they had indeed found a photograph behind a Turner in the National Gallery at 5.15 that morning. It was tucked behind *Ulysses Deriding Polyphemus* (No.508). He went on in his court-room voice –

'The photograph depicts, ah, two consenting adult males, ah, consenting.'

'Having congress, you mean?'

'Just so.'

'And one of the faces had been cut out?'

'Both of the faces.'

I got up and went over to where my hat was. The two louts did not move but looked sort of alert. I was not really in any shape to dive out of windows. I pulled down the sweatband of the hat, tore back some of the buckram and offered Martland the tiny oval of photograph. He looked at it blankly.

'Well, dear boy,' he said softly, 'you mustn't keep us in suspense. Who is the gentleman?'

It was my turn to look blank.

'Don't you really know?'

He looked at it again.

'Much hairier in the face nowadays,' I prompted.

He shook his head.

'Chap called Gloag,' I told him. 'Known to his friends as "Hockbottle" for some obscene reason. He took the photograph himself. At Cambridge.'

Martland, suddenly, inexplicably, looked very worried indeed. So did his mates, who clustered around, passing the tiny picture from hand to grubby hand. Then they all started nodding, tentatively at first and then positively. They looked rather funny but I was feeling too tired to enjoy it really.

Martland wheeled on me, his face evil now.

'Come on, Mortdecai,' he said, all urbanity gone, 'tell me it all this time. Fast, before I lose my temper.'

'Sandwich?' I asked diffidently. 'Bottle of beer?'

'Later.'

'Oh. All right Hockbottle Gloag came to see me three weeks ago. He gave me the cut-out of his face and said to keep it very safe, it was a free pardon for him and money in the bank for me. He wouldn't explain but I knew he wouldn't be trying to con me, he's terrified of Jock. He said he'd ring me up every day from then on and if he missed a day it would mean he was in trouble and I was to tell you to ask Turner in the National Gallery. That's all. It has nothing to do with the Goya so far as I know – I just seized that opportunity to slip you the word. *Is* Hockbottle in trouble? Have you got him in that bloody Cottage Hospital of yours?'

Martland didn't answer. He just stood looking at me, rubbing the side of his face, making a nasty soft rasping sound. I could almost hear him wondering whether the battery would coax a little more truth out of me. I hoped not: the truth had to be delivered in carefully spaced rations, so as to give him a healthy appetite for later lies.

Perhaps he decided that I was telling the truth, as far as it went; perhaps he simply decided that he already had enough to worry about.

He had, in fact, no idea how much he had to worry about.

'Go away,' he said, finally.

I collected my hat, tidied it, made for the door.

'Don't leave town?' I prompted in the doorway.

'Don't leave town,' he agreed, absently. I didn't like to remind him about the sandwich.

I had to walk miles before I found a taxi. It had all its door handles. I fell soundly asleep, the sleep of a good, successful liar. Goodness, the flat was in a mess. I telephoned Mrs Spon and told her that I was at last ready to redecorate. She came round before dinner and helped us tidy the place up – success has not spoiled her – and afterward we spent a happy hour in front of the fire choosing chintzes and wallpapers and things and then we all three sat round the kitchen table and tore into an enormous fry-up such as very few people can make today.

After Mrs Spon had left I said to Jock, 'Do you know what, Jock?' and he said, 'No, what?'

'I think Mr Gloag is dead.'

'Greedy, I expect,' said Jock, elliptically. 'Who d'you reckon killed him, then?'

'Mr Martland, I fancy. But I think that for once he rather wishes he hadn't.'

'Eh?'

'Yes. Well, good night, Jock.'

'Good night, Mr Charlie.'

I undressed and put a little more Pomade Divine on my wounds. Suddenly I felt shatteringly tired – I always do after torture. Jock had put a hotty in my bed, bless him. He knows.

3

Yet half I seemed to recognize some trick
Of mischief happened to me, God knows when –
In a bad dream perhaps. Here ended, then,
Progress this way. When, in the very nick
Of giving up, one time more, came a click
As when a trap shuts – you're inside the den!

Childe Roland

Dawn broke for me, at ten o'clock sharp, with one of the finest cups
of tea I have ever been privileged to toy with. The canary was in
splendid voice. The snail, once again, was on the thorn and showed
no signs of dismounting. I hardly winced as the blisters from
Martland's battery made themselves felt, although I did, at one stage,
find myself longing for Pantagruel's goose's neck.

I had a long chat on the telephone with my insurance brokers and
explained to them how they could put the bite on Martland's ear for
the damage to my decorations and promised them the photographs of
the intruders as soon as Jock had developed them.

Then I put on a dashing little tropical-weight worsted, a curly-
brimmed coker and a pair of buckskins created by Lobb in a moment
of genius. (My tie, if I recall correctly, was a *foulard*, predominantly
merde d'oie in colour, though why you should be interested I cannot
imagine.) Thus clad – and with my blisters well Vaselined – I sauntered to the Park to inspect the pelican and other feathered friends.
They were in great shape. 'This weather,' they seemed to be saying,
'is capital.' I gave them my benison.

Then I went a-slumming through the art-dealing district, carefully
keeping my face straight as I looked in the shop windows – sorry,

gallery windows – at the tatty Shayers and reach-me-down
Koekkoeks. Heigh-ho. After a while I was sure that I had no tail
(remember that bit, it matters) neither in front nor behind, and popped
into Mason's Yard. There are galleries there too, of course, but I was
bent on seeing Mr Spinoza, who is only an art dealer in one very spe-
cialized sort of way.

Moishe Spinoza Barzilai is, as a matter of fact, Basil Wayne & Co.,
the great coach builders of whom even you, ignorant readers, must
have heard, although not point one per cent of you will ever afford his
lovely panel beating, still less his princely upholstery. Unless, of
course, you are reading below your station in life and happen to be an
Indian Maharajah or a Texan oil-field proprietor.

Mr Spinoza creates very special one-off bodies for the great cars
of the world. He has heard of Hooper and Mulliner and speaks kindly,
if a little vaguely, of them. He will restore or re-create the occasional
vintage Rolls, Infanta or Mercedes if he feels like it. Bugattis, Cords,
Hirondelles and Leyland Straight-Eights will be considered. So will
about three other *marques*. But ask him to tart up a Mini with basket-
work and silver condom dispensers or to build flip-back fornication
benches into a Jaguar and he will spit right into your eye. I mean *really!*
What he most loves is a Hispano-Suiza – an 'Izzer-Swizzer.' Can't
understand it myself, but there.

He also dabbles in crime. It's a sort of hobby with him. He can't
need the money.

Currently, he was rebuilding for my best customer a latish Silver
Ghost Rolls Royce, which was what I had come to inspect, in a way.
My customer, Milton Krampf (yes, truly), had bought it from a right
villain who had found it in a farmyard chocked up and running a chaff
cutter and turnip slicer after a long career as stock truck, hearse, station wagon, shooting brake, baronial wedding present and mobile
shagging station; in the reverse order, of course. Mr Spinoza had
found six perfectly right artillery wheels for it at one hundred pounds
apiece, had built a scrupulously exact *Roi des Belges* open tourer
body and painted it with sixteen coats of Queen Anne white, each one
rubbed down wet-and-dry, and was now finishing the olive-green
crushed Levant Morocco upholstery and free-handing with the fitch

the lovely arabesques of the *carrosserie* lines. He wasn't doing the work himself, of course; he's blind. Was, rather.

I walked round the car, admiring it Platonically. There was no point in desiring it – it was a rich man's car. Would do about seven miles to the gallon, which is all right if you own an oil field. Milton Krampf owns a lot of oil fields. First to last, the car would stand him in at about £24,000. Paying that would hurt him about as much as picking his nose. (They say a man who knows how rich he is ain't rich – well, Krampf knows. A man telephones him every morning, one hour after the New York Stock Exchange opens, and tells him exactly how rich he is. It makes his day.)

A naughty apprentice told me that Mr Spinoza was in his office and I picked my way thither.

'Hullo, Mr Spinoza,' I cried cheerily, 'here's a fine morning to be alive in!'

He peered malevolently at a spot three inches above my left shoulder.

'Oo hucking hastard,' he spat. (No roof to his mouth, you know. Poor chap.) 'Oo other hucking hiss-hot. How air oo hoe your hace here, oo hurd-murgling hod?'

The rest was a bit rude so I shan't quote him too verbatim, if you don't mind. What he was vexed about was my sending the MGB in with the little special matter in the headcloth at such an early hour the day before. 'At sparrow-fart,' as he neatly put it. Moreover, he was afraid that people would think he was working on it and he had evolved a dreadful mental image of queues of chaps in cloth caps insisting that he respray their MG's.

When he had drawn to a provisional close, I spoke to him sternly.

'Mr Spinoza,' I said, 'I did not come here to discuss with you my relationship with my mummy, which is a matter for me and my psychiatrist alone. I came to remonstrate with you about using Dirty Words to Jock, who is, as you know, sensitive.'

Mr S used a lot more *very* dirty words and some which I couldn't make out but which were probably vile. When the air had thinned a little he bitterly offered to walk over to the Rolls with me and discuss headlamps. I was surprised and saddened to see a great vulgar

Duesenburg – if that's how you spell it – in the workshop, and said so, which rather started him off again. I have never had any daughters but this did not stop Mr Spinoza sketching out their careers from the nursery to the street corner, so to speak. I leaned on the side of the Silver Ghost, admiring his command of language. 'A feast of reason and a flow of soul' is how Alexander Pope (1688–1744) would have summed it up.

While we were thus civilly biffing the ball of conversation to and fro, a sound which I can best describe as a DONK came in from the South side of Mason's Yard. More or less simultaneously a sort of WANG occurred about three feet north of my belly button and a large pimple appeared in the door-panel of the Silver Ghost. Slapping two and two together in the twinkling of an eye, I lay down, without a thought for my valuable suit. Look, I'm an experienced coward. Mr Spinoza, whose hand had been on the door, realized that someone was getting at his panel work. He straightened up and cried 'Oi!' or it might have been 'Oy!'

There was another DONK outside, followed, this time, not by a WANG but by a sort of crisp, mushy noise and a lot of the back of Mr Spinoza's head distributed itself freely over the wall behind us. None of it got on to my suit, I'm happy to say. Mr Spinoza, too, lay down then, but too late by now, of course. There was a blue-black hole in his upper lip and a piece of his false teeth arrangements was protruding from the corner of his mouth. He looked quite beastly.

I wish I could say that I had liked him, but I never really did, you know.

Gentlemen of my age and full habit (as the tailors say) almost never scuttle on all fours over oily garage floors, particularly when they are wearing expensive and rather new tropical-weight worsted suitings. This was clearly a day for breaking rules, however, so I put my nose down and scuttled, successfully. I must have looked absurd but I got out into the yard and across it into the doorway of the O'Flaherty Gallery. Mr O'Flaherty, who knew my father well, is an elderly Jew called Groenblatter or something like that and is swart as an Ethiop. He put his hands to his cheeks when he saw me and rocked his head to and fro, keening something that sounded like *Mmm-Mmm-Mmmm* on the note of G above high C.

'How's business today?' I asked bravely but in a voice that wobbled a bit.

'Don't ask it, don't ask it,' he replied automatically, then –

'Who attacked you so, Charlie boy, somebody's husband? Or somebody's wife, God forbid?'

'Look, Mr G, nobody attacked me, there's some sort of trouble at Mr Spinoza's and I'm getting away fast – who wants to be involved – when I trip and fall, is all. Now like a good friend you should ask Perce to get me a taxi arreddy, I don't feel so good.' I always find myself talking like that with Mr G.

Perce, Mr G's rat-faced little thug – he can't afford a good, big one – got the taxi and I promised to send Mr G a good customer, which I knew would keep him from gossiping.

Arrived home, I collapsed into a chair, suddenly quaking with delayed horror. Jock made me a cup of wonderfully refreshing mint tea which made me feel a great deal better, especially after I had followed it with four fluid ozs of whisky.

Jock pointed out that if I said I'd been knocked down by a motor car the Insurance would buy me a new suit. This completed the cure and I got on to the brokers straight away, for my no-claims bonus is just a dream of childhood now. There's nothing like a little insurance to smooth the troubled brow, take my word for it. Meanwhile, Jock sent the porter's little girl to Prunier in a taxi for a box of luncheon *à porter*. There was a dear little turbot *soufflé*, a *Varieté Prunier* (six oysters, each cooked a different way) and two of their *petits pots de crème de chocolat*.

I had a nap and awoke much mollified and spent a useful afternoon with my ultra-violet machine and a grease crayon, mapping the passages of repaint ('strengthening' as we call it in on a gorgeous panel by – well, more or less by – the Allunno di Amico di Sandro. (God bless Berenson, I say.) Then I wrote a few paragraphs of my paper for *Burlington Magazine* in which I shall prove, once and for all, that the Tallard Madonna in the Ashmolean is by Giorgione after all, and despite that awful man Berenson.

Dinner was pork chops with the kidneys in and chips and beer. I always send Jock out for the beer in a jug and make him wear a cloth cap. It seems to taste better and he doesn't mind a bit. They won't serve the porter's little girl, you see.

After dinner Mrs Spon arrived with lots of samples of gimp and bobbles and crétonnes for cushion covers and things and pink mosquito netting for the standing drapes round my bed. I had to be firm about the netting, I must admit it was rather lovely but I insisted that it should be blue-for-a-boy. I mean, I have my little ways but I'm not a deviate, for God's sake, am I, I asked her.

She was already just a little cross when Martland arrived and loomed in the doorway like a pollution problem. Diffidently, for him, but definitely doomlike.

They admitted, grudgingly, that they knew each other by sight. Mrs Spon flounced over to the window. I know lots of men who can flounce but Mrs Spon is the last woman who can do it. There was a sticky sort of silence of the sort which I relish. Finally Martland whispered, 'Perhaps you should ask the old doxy to leave' in just too loud a whisper.

Mrs Spon rounded on him and Told Him Off. I had heard of her talents in that direction but had never before been privileged to hear her unlock the word bag. It was a literary and emotional feast: Martland withered visibly. There is no one like your gently nurtured triple-divorcee for really putting the verbal leather in. 'Wart on the tax-payer's arse,' 'traffic-warden's catamite,' and 'poor man's Colonel Wigg' are just a few of the good things she served up but there was more – much more. She swept out at last, in a cloud of *Ragazza* and lovely epithets. She was wearing a suede knickerbocker suit but you'd have sworn she twitched a twelve-foot train of brocade away from Martland as she passed him.

'Golly,' he said when she'd gone.

'Yes,' I said, happily.

'Well. Well, look, Charlie, what I really came to say was how sick and sorry I am about all this.'

I gave him my cold look. The big, economy size.

'I mean,' he went on, 'you've had a filthy rotten time and I think you're owed an explanation. I want to put you in the picture – which will give you a bit of a whip-hand, I don't mind telling you – and er ask your er help.'

'Gor blimey,' I thought.

'Sit down,' I said, frigidly. 'I myself prefer to stand, for reasons which will occur to you. I shall certainly listen to your explanations and apologies; beyond that I can make no promises.'

'Yes,' he said. He fidgeted a little, like a man who is expecting to be offered a drink and thinks you've forgotten to do the honours. When he realized that it was definitely Temperance Night for him he resumed.

'Do you know why Spinoza was shot this morning?'

'Haven't the faintest,' I said boredly, although a multiplicity of ideas about it had been running through my head all afternoon. Wrong ones.

'It was meant for you, Charlie.'

My heart started rattling about irresponsibly in my rib cage. My armpits became cold and wet. I wanted to go to the lavatory.

I mean, electric batteries and so forth are one thing, within reason of course, but that someone actually means to kill you, forever, is a thought that the mind cannot accept, it wants to vomit it out; ordinary people just don't have the mental or emotional clichés to deal with news like that.

'How can you possibly be sure of that?' I asked after a moment.

'Well, to be perfectly frank, Maurice thought it was you he shot. It was certainly you he meant to shoot.'

'Maurice?' I said. '*Maurice?* You mean *your* Maurice? Whatever would he want to do that for?'

'Well, I sort of told him to, really.'

I sat down after all.

Jock's craggy form disengaged itself smoothly from the shadows just outside the door and came to rest behind my chair. He was breathing through his nose for once, making a plaintive, whistling noise on the exhaust stroke.

'Did you ring, Sir?'

Jock really is marvellous. I mean, imagine saying that. What tact,

what *savoir faire*, what a boost for the young master in time of stress.
I felt so much better.

'Jock,' I said, 'have you a pair of brass knuckles about you? I may
ask you to hit Mr Martland in a moment or two.'

Jock didn't actually answer, he knows a rhetorical question when
he hears one. But I sensed him pat his hip pocket – 'me bin' he calls
it – where six ounces of cunningly fashioned brass have lived a snug
and smelly life since he was the youngest juvenile delinquent in
Hoxton.

Martland was shaking his head vigorously, impatiently 'No need
for that at all, none at all. Try and understand, Charlie.'

'Try and make me understand,' I said. Grim, sore-arsed.

He heaved what I took to be a sigh. *'Tout comprendre, c'est tout
pardonner,'* he said.

'I say, that's neat!'

'Look, Charlie, I was up half the night with that bloodthirsty little
old maniac at the Home Office, telling him about our chat yesterday.'

'Chat' was good.

'When I told him how much you knew about this file,' Martland
went on, 'nothing would do but he must have you done permanently.
"Terminated with extreme prejudice" was how he put it, silly little
sod. Been reading too many thrillers in between the cups of tea.'

'No,' I said kindly, 'that one hasn't got into the thrillers yet, except
the *Sunday Times*. That's CIA jargon. He's probably been reading the
Green Berets file.'

'Be that as it may,' he went on, 'be that as it may' – he obviously
fancied that snappy little phrase – 'be that as it may, I tried to make
him see that as yet we really didn't know what you knew nor where
you got it, which was more important; and that it would be madness to
liquidate you at this stage. Er, or at any stage of course, but I couldn't
say that, could I? Well, I tried to get him to refer it to the Minister
but he said the Minister would be drunk by then and he himself
wasn't permanent enough to disturb him with impunity at that time
of night and anyway . . . anyway I had to come into line and so
this morning I thought the best thing was to put Maurice on the
assignment, being an impulsive boy, and so give you a fair chance of

survival, you see. And Charlie, I'm really so glad that he got the wrong chap.'

'Yes,' I said. But I wondered how he had known that I would be at Mr Spinoza's that morning.

'How did you know that I would be at Mr Spinoza's this morning?' I asked, casually.

'Maurice followed you, Charlie.' Wide-eyed, offhand.

'Bloody liar,' I thought.

'I see,' I said.

I excused myself on the pretext of slipping into something more comfortable, as the tarts say. Something more comfortable was a wonderfully vulgar blue velvet smoking jacket into which Mrs Spon had once sewn, with her own hands, a lot of cunningly designed webbing which supported a rather shaky old gold-plated riverboat gambler's revolver, calibre something like .28. I had only eleven of the ancient pinfire cartridges for it and had grave doubts of their usefulness, not to speak of their safety. But this wasn't for killing anyone, it was for making me feel young and tough and capable. People who have pistols for killing people keep them in boxes or drawers; wearing them is only for making you ride tall in the saddle. I used some mouthwash, renewed the Vaseline on my blisters and cantered back into the drawing room, tall as can be in my high-cantled saddle.

I paused behind Martland's chair and reflected on how much I disliked the back of his head. It wasn't that there were rolls of Teuton fat sprouting hog bristles or anything like that; just a neat and hateful smugness, an unjustified but invincible cockiness. Like a female journalist, really. I decided that I could afford the luxury of losing my temper: it would fit into the picture I wanted to create. I took out the little pistol and ground the muzzle into his right ear hole. He sat very still indeed – nothing really wrong with his nerves – and spoke plaintively.

'For Christ's sake be careful with that thing, Charlie, those pinfire cartridges are highly unstable.'

I ground some more; it was making my blisters feel better. It was just like him to have been looking at my firearm permit.

'Jock,' I said crisply, 'we are going to defenestrate Mr Martland.'

Jock's eyes lit up.

'I'll get a razor blade, Mr Charlie.'

'No no, Jock, wrong word. I mean we're going to push him out of a window. Your bedroom window, I think. Yes, and we'll undress him first and say that he was making advances to you and jumped out of the window in a frenzy of thwarted love.'

'I say, Charlie, really, what a filthy rotten idea; I mean, think of my wife.'

'I never think of policemen's wives, their beauty maddens me like wine. Anyway, the sodomy bit will make your Minister slap a D-Notice on the whole thing, which is good for both of us.'

Jock was already leading him from the room by means of the 'Quiet Come-Along' which painfully involves the victim's little finger. Jock had learned that one from a mental nurse. Capable lads, those.

Jock's bedroom, as ever, was bursting with what passes for fresh air in W.I, the stuff was streaming in from the wide-open window. (Why do people build houses to keep the climate out, then cut holes in the walls to let it in again? I shall never understand.)

'Show Mr Martland the spiky railings in the area, Jock,' I said nastily. (You've no idea how nasty my voice can be when I try. I was an adjutant once, in your actual Guards.) Jock held him out so that he could see the railings then started to undress him. He just stood there, unresisting, a shaky smile trembling at one corner of his mouth, until Jock began to unbuckle his belt. Then he started to talk, rapidly.

The burden of his song was that if I could only be dissuaded from my course he would arrange for me to receive

(i) the untold riches of the Orient

(ii) his undying respect and esteem and

(iii) legal immunity for me and mine, yea, even unto the third and fourth generations. At this point I cocked an ear. (How I wish I could really move my ears, don't you? The Bursar of my College could.)

'You interest me strangely,' I said. 'Put him down a moment, Jock, for he is going to Tell All.'

We didn't lay another finger on him, he went on and on of his own accord. You don't have to be a coward to dislike dropping thirty feet on to spiky railings, especially in the nude. I'm sure that in his place I'd have blubbered.

The story so far turned out to be as follows, to wit: Hockbottle Gloag, with an extraordinary lack of finesse, had put the bite directly onto the ear of his old College Chum – the other part of the 'consenting males' sketch – sending him a 35-mm contact print of the naughty photograph. (This was by no means part of the agreed plan and was very vexing. I suppose he needed spending money, poor chap; I wish he'd asked me.) The now very august chum, living in dread of his wife's Sister and other Relations, had decided to cough up the reasonable sum involved but had also asked an Assistant Commissioner of Police to dinner and had put out dainty feelers over the port, such as, 'What do you fellows do about blackmailers nowadays, eh, Freddy?' and so forth. The Assistant Commissioner, who had seen certain unpublished material about the Chum in a newspaper editor's safe, shied like a startled stallion. Decided that it wasn't anything he could afford to know about and – perhaps spitefully – gave Chum the name and number of old Martland. 'Just in case anyone you know ever gets pestered, Sir, ha ha.'

Chummy then asks Martland to dinner and gives him all the news that's fit to print. Martland says, 'Leave it to us, Sir, we're used to dealing with dastards of that kidney,' and swings into action.

Next day, some sort of equerry, snorting genteelly into his Squadron-Leading moustaches, calls on Hockbottle and hands him over an attaché case full of great coarse ten-pound notes. Five minutes later, Martland and his gauleiters canter in and whisk poor Hockbottle off to the Cottage Hospital of evil fame. He gets a touch of the car battery just to soften him up and comes out of his faint with the regulation glass of Scotch under his nose. But he is made of sterner stuff than me: your actual boofter often is.

'Faugh,' he says, or it might have been 'Pooh!' petulantly; 'take the nasty stuff away. Have you no Chartreuse? And you needn't think you're frightening me: I *adore* being roughed up by great big hairy dears like you.' He proves it, shows them. They are revolted.

Now Martland's brief is only to put the fear of God into Hockbottle and to make it clear that this photograph nuisance must now cease. He has been specifically ordered not to pry and has been told nothing embarrassing, but by nature and long habit he is nosy and has, moreover, a quite unwholesome horror of pooves. He decides to get to the bottom of the mystery (an unfortunate expression perhaps) and to make Hockbottle Tell All.

'Very well,' he says grimly, 'this one will really hurt you.'

'Promises, promises,' simpers Hockbottle.

So now they give him a treatment which hurts you at the base of the septum and this is one which even Hockbottle is unlikely to relish. When he regains consciousness this time, he is very angry and also scared of losing his good looks, and he tells Martland that he has some very powerful insurance c/o the Hon. Charlie Mortdecai and they'd better look out, so there. He then shuts up firmly and Martland, now enraged, gives him yet another treatment, hitherto reserved solely for Chinese double agents. Hockbottle, to everyone's dismay, drops dead. Dicky ticker, d'you see.

Well, worse things happen in war, as they say, and no one ever really liked Hockbottle of course, except perhaps a few Guardsmen from Chelsea Barracks, but Martland is not a man who appreciates uncovenanted mercies. The whole thing strikes him as thoroughly unsatisfactory, especially since he still has not found out what it is all about.

Judge of his chagrin then, when Chum telephones in a serious tizzy and asks him to call round immediately, bringing the wretched Hockers with him. Martland says yes, certainly, he'll be there in a few minutes but it's a little er difficult to bring Mr er Gloag just at present. When he arrives he is shown, distraughtly, a most distressing letter. Even Martland, whose taste has a few little blemishes in it, boggles at the paper it is written on: imitation parchment with edges both deckled and gilt, richly embossed bogus coat of arms at the top and a polychrome view of a desert sunset at the foot of the page. The address, inscribed in Olde Englysshe lettering, is *'Rancho de los Siete Dolores de la Virgen,'* New Mexico. In short, it is from my very good customer Milton Krampf.

The letter says – mind you, I never saw it, so I'm paraphrasing Martland's account – that Mr Krampf admires the eminent Chum very much and wants to start a fan club (!) to distribute little known biographical material about said Chum to Senators, Congressmen, British MP's and *Paris Match*. (Terrifying, that last bit, you will admit.) He further says that a Mr Hogwattle Gloat has been in touch with him and is prepared to kick in with some illustrated reminiscences of 'your mutual schooldays in Cambridge'. He also says how about the three of them meeting someplace and seeing if they can't work out something to their mutual advantages. In other words, it is the bite. Coy and clumsy perhaps, but unmistakably the bite. (That made, so far, two members of the cast who'd gone off their chumps, leaving only me sane and responsible. I think.)

Martland paused in his narrative and I did not urge him on, for this was very bad news, for when millionaires go mad poorer people get hurt. I was so disturbed that I unthinkingly gave Martland a drink. A bad mistake that, I needed him to stay on edge. As he filled with the old familiar juice you could see his confidence returning, has head reassuming the habitual, maddeningly pompous poise. How he must have been loathed by his brother officers as they watched him bully and arsehole-creep his way up the service. But one had to remember, all the time, that he was dangerous and far cleverer than he looked or talked.

'Martland,' I said after a time, 'did you say that your hirelings followed me to Spinoza's this morning?'

'That's right.' Crisply, much too crisply. He was definitely feeling his oats again.

'Jock, Mr Martland is telling me fibs. Smack him, please.'

Jock drifted out of the shadows, gently relieved Martland of his glass and bent down to stare benignly into his face. Martland stared back, wide-eyed, his mouth opening a little. A mistake that, the open mouth. Jock's great hand swung round in a half circle and struck Martland's cheek with a loud report.

Martland sailed over the arm of the sofa and fetched up against the wainscot. He sat there a while; his little eyes dripping tears of hatred and funk. His mouth, closed now, writhed – he was counting his teeth, I expect.

'I think that perhaps that was silly of me,' I said. 'I mean, killing you is safe enough, it sort of ties things up for good, doesn't it, but just hurting you will only make you vengeful.' I let him think about that for a time, to get the nasty implications. He thought about it. He got them.

At last he cranked a sickly smirk on to his face – beastly sight, that – and came and sat down again.

'I shan't bear a grudge, Charlie. I dare say you feel I deserve a bit of a bashing after this morning. Not yourself yet, I mean to say.'

'There is something in what you say,' I said, truthfully, for there was something in what he said. 'I have had a long day, full of mopery and mayhem. If I stay up any longer I am likely to make a serious error of judgment. Goodnight.' With this I swept out of the room. Martland's mouth was open again as I closed the door.

A brief, delicious session under the warm shower, a whisk of costly dentifrice around the old ivory castles, a puff of Johnson's Baby Powder here and there, a dive between the sheets and I was my own man again. Krampf's idiotic departure from his script worried me, perhaps more than the attempt on my own life now, but I felt that there was nothing which could not more profitably be worried about on the morrow which is, as is well known, another day.

I rinsed the cares from my mind with a few pages of Firbank and swam gently and tenderly down into sleep. Sleep is not, with me, a mere switching off: it is a very positive pleasure to be supped and savoured with expertise. It was a good night; sleep pampered me like a familiar, salty mistress who yet always has a new delight with which to surprise her jaded lover.

My blisters, too, were much better.

4

Morning's at seven,
The hill-side's dew-pearled,
                    Pippa Passes

I carolled at Jock as he aroused me, but my heart wasn't really in the
statement. Morning was in fact at ten, as usual, and Upper Brook
Street was merely wet. It was a gritty, drizzling, clammy day and the
sky was the colour of mouse dirt. Pippa would have stayed in bed and
no snail in his senses would have climbed a thorn. My cup of tea,
which usually droppeth like the gentle rain from heaven, tasted like a
vulture's crutch. The canary looked constipated and gave me a surly
glance instead of the customary stave or two of song.

'Mr Martland's downstairs, Mr Charlie. Bin waiting half an hour.'

I snarled and drew a fold of silk sheet over my head, burrowing
down back into the womby warmth where no one can hurt you.

'You ought to see his moosh, where I hit him, it's a treat, honest.
All colours.'

That fetched me. The day had at least one treat to offer. Against my
better judgment I got up.

A mouth wash, half a dexedrine, a morsel of anchovy toast and a
Charvet dressing-gown – all in the order named – and I was ready to
deal with any number of Martlands.

'Lead me to this Martland,' I ordered.

I must say he did look lovely; it wasn't just the rich autumnal tints
on his swollen moosh, it was the play of expressions over it which
enchanted me. You may compile your own list of these; I have no
heart for it just now. The one which matters for this narrative was
the last: a kind of sheepish false bonhomie with a careful dash of

wryness, like two drops of Worcester sauce in a plate of gravy soup.

He bounced up and strode toward me, face first, hand outstretched for a manly grip.

'Friends again, Charlie?' he mumbled.

It was my turn to drop the lower jaw – I broke out in a sweat of embarrassment and shame for the man. Well, I mean. I made a sort of gruff, gargling noise which seemed to satisfy him for he dropped my hand and settled back cosily on to the sofa. To hide my nonplussedness I ordered Jock to make coffee for us.

We waited for the coffee in silence, more or less. Martland tried a weather gambit – he's one of those people who always know when the latest V-shaped depression is likely to emerge from its roost over Iceland. I explained kindly that until I had drunk coffee of a morning I was a poor judge of meteorology.

(What is the origin of this strange British preoccupation with the weather? How can adult male Empire-builders gravely discuss whether or no it is raining, has rained or is likely to rain? Can you imagine the most barren-minded Parisian, Viennese or Berliner demeaning himself by talking such piffle? *'Ils sont fous ces Bretons,'* says Obelix, rightly. I suppose it is really just another manifestation of the Englishman's fantasy about the soil. The most urbane cit is, in his inner heart, a yeoman farmer and yearns for leather gaiters and a shotgun.)

The coffee having arrived (how hard it is to write without the ablative absolute!) we guzzled genteelly for a while, passing each other sugar and cream and things and beaming falsely from time to time. Then I lowered the boom.

'You were going to tell me how you knew I was at Spinoza's,' I said.

'Charlie, why ever are you so fascinated by that particular detail?'

It was a very good question indeed, but one which I had no intention of answering. I stared at him blankly.

'Oh, well, it's quite simple really. We happen to know that old Spinoza has – had, rather – about a quarter of a million grubby pound notes from the Great Train job. He paid for them in clean fivers and got a hundred and seventy-five pounds per cent. Bloody old crook.

Well, we knew he would be having to unload soon so we hired a little yob who works for one of the galleries in Mason's Yard to watch the place for us. Anyone, well, interesting, goes to see Spinoza, we get the word on our yob's little walkie-talkie.'

'Really,' I said. 'Now I do call that riveting. What about callers before gallery hours?'

'Ah, yes, well, there we have to take a chance, of course. I mean, there just aren't funds to run shifts on all these jobs. Cost a fortune.'

I made a mental 'whew' of relief, believing him. A thought struck me.

'Martland, is your nark a little tit called Perce, works for the O'Flaherty Gallery?'

'Well, yes, I think that is his name, as a matter of fact.'

'Just so,' I said.

I cocked an ear, Jock was outside the door, breathing through his nose, making mental notes, if you can properly call them that. There's no doubt that I was much relieved to learn that only Perce was suborned; had Mr Spinoza been playing the strumpet with me all would have been lost. In spades. I must have allowed my expression to relax for I realized that Martland was looking at me curiously. This would not do. Change the subject.

'Well now,' I cried heartily, 'what's the deal? Where are these riches of the Orient you were pressing upon me last night? "Nay, even unto half your kingdom" was the sum mentioned, I believe?'

'Oh, really, come now Charlie, last night was last night, wasn't it? I mean, we were both a bit overwrought, weren't we? You're surely not holding me to that.'

'The window is still there,' I said simply, 'and so is Jock. And I may say that I am still overwrought; no one has ever tried to murder me in cold blood before.'

'But obviously I've taken precautions this time, haven't I?' he said, and he patted a hip pocket. This told me that his pistol, if anywhere, was under his armpit, of course.

'Let us play a game, Martland. If you can get that thing out before Jock hits you on the head, you win the coconut.'

'Oh come on, Charlie, let's stop sodding about. I'm quite prepared to offer you substantial ah benefits and ah concessions if you'll play along with our side over this business. You know damn well I'm in the shit and if I can't recruit you that awful old man in the Home Office will be baying for your blood again. What will you settle for? I'm sure you aren't interested in the sort of money my department can offer.'

'I think I'd like a Bonzo dog.'

'Oh God, Charlie, can't you be serious?'

'No, really, a greyhound; you know, a silver one.'

'You can't mean you want to be a Queen's Messenger? What in God's name for? And what makes you think I could swing that?'

I said, 'First, yes, I do; second, mind your own business; third, you can swing it if you have to. I also want the diplomatic passport that goes with it and the privilege of taking a diplomatic bag to the Embassy in Washington.'

He leaned back in his chair, all knowing and relaxed now. 'And what is likely to be in the bag, or is that not my business either?'

'A Rolls Royce, as a matter of fact. Well, it won't actually be in a bag, of course, but it will be smothered in diplomatic seals. Same thing.'

He looked grave, worried; his under-engined brain revving furiously as its *deux chevaux* tried to cope with this gradient.

'Charlie, if it's going to be full of drugs the answer is no repeat no. If it's grubby pound notes in a reasonable quantity I might see my way, but I don't think I could protect you afterwards.'

'It is neither,' I said firmly. 'On my word of honour.' I looked him squarely and frankly in the eye as I said it, so that he would be sure that I was lying. (Those notes from the Train will have to be changed soon, won't they?) He eyed me back like a trusting comrade, then carefully placed all ten fingertips together, eyeing them with modest pride as though he'd done something clever. He was thinking hard and didn't care who knew it.

'Well, I suppose something on those lines could be worked out,' he said at last. 'You realize, of course, that the degree of co-operation expected from you would have to be proportionate to the difficulty of getting you what you ask?'

'Oh yes,' I replied brightly, 'you will want me to kill Mr Krampf, won't you?'

'Yes, that's right. How did you guess?'

'Well, clearly, now that Hockbottle has been, er, terminated, you can't possibly leave Krampf alive, knowing what he does, can you? And I may say it's a bit rough on me because he happens to be a rather good customer of mine.'

'Yes, I know.'

'Yes, I thought you would know by now. Otherwise I probably wouldn't have mentioned it, ha ha.'

'Ha ha.'

'Anyway, it's clear that you can't put any pressure on a chap as rich as Krampf except by killing him. It's also clear that I can get close to him and that getting me to do it will save your estimates a fortune. Moreover, no one could possibly be as expendable as me from your point of view – and I can scarcely be traced to any official agency. Lastly, if I do it clumsily and get myself into an electric chair you've killed both Krampf and me with one gallstone.'

'Well, some of that's more or less true,' he said.

'Yes,' I said.

Then I sat at my silly little French desk – the one the witty dealer called a *malheur-du-jour* because he paid too much for it – and wrote a list of all the things I wanted Martland to do. It was quite long. His face darkened as he read but he bore it like a little man and tucked the paper carefully in his wallet. I noticed that he was not wearing a shoulder holster after all, but that had not been my first mistake that day by any means.

The coffee was by now cold and horrid, so I courteously gave him what was left of it. I daresay he didn't notice. Then he left after a chummy commonplace or two; for a moment I feared he was going to shake my hand again.

'Jock,' I said, 'I am going back to bed. Be so kind as to bring me all the London telephone books, a shakerful of cocktails – any sort, let it be a surprise – and several watercress sandwiches made of soft white bread.'

Bed is the only place for protracted telephoning. It is also excellently suited to reading, sleeping and listening to canaries. It is not at all a good place for sex: sex should take place in armchairs, or in bathrooms, or on lawns which have been brushed but not too recently mown, or on sandy beaches if you happen to have been circumcised. If you are too tired to have intercourse except in bed you are probably too tired anyway and should be husbanding your strength. Women are the great advocates of sex in bed because they have bad figures to hide (usually) and cold feet to warm (always). Boys are different, of course. But you probably knew that. I must try not to be didactic.

After an hour I arose, draped the person in whipcord and hopsack and descended to the kitchen to give the canary one more chance to be civil to me. It was more than civil, almost busting its tiny gut with song, vowing that all would yet be well. I accepted its assurances guardedly.

Calling for coat and hat I tripped downstairs – I never use the lift on Saturdays, it's my day for exercise. (Well, I use it going *up*, naturally.)

The concierge emerged from her lair and gibbered at me: I silenced her with a finger to my lips and significantly raised eyebrows. Never fails. She slunk back, mopping and mowing.

I walked all the way to Sotheby's, holding my tummy in nearly the whole time, terribly good for one. There was a picture belonging to me in the sale, a tiny canvas of a Venetian nobleman's barge with livened gondoliers and a wonderfully blue sky. I had bought it months before, hoping to persuade myself that it was by Longhi, but my efforts had been in vain so I had put it into Sotheby's, who had austerely called it 'Venetian School, XVIII Century.' I ran it up to the figure I had paid for it, then left it to its own devices. To my delight it ran for another three hundred and fifty before being knocked down to a man I detest. It is probably in a Duke Street window this moment, labelled Marieschi or some such nonsense. I stayed another ten minutes and spent my profit on a doubtful but splendidly naughty Bartolomaeus Spränger showing Mars diddling Venus with his helmet on – such *manners*! On my way out of the Rooms I telephoned a rich turkey farmer in Suffolk and sold him the Spränger, sight unseen, for what is known as an undisclosed sum, and toddled righteously away towards Piccadilly. There's nothing like a little dealing to buck one up.

Across Piccadilly without so much as a bad fright, through Fortnum's for the sake of the lovely smells, a step along Jermyn Street and I was snug in Jules's Bar, ordering luncheon and blotting up my fifth White Lady. (I forgot to tell you what Jock's surprise had been; sorry.) As a serious gastronome I deplore cocktails of course, but then I also deplore dishonesty, promiscuity, inebriety and many another goody.

If anyone had been following me hitherto they were welcome, I'm sure. For the afternoon, however, I needed privacy from the SPG boys so I scanned the room carefully from time to time as I ate. By closing time the whole population of the bar had changed except for one or two permanent fixtures whom I knew by sight: if there had been a tail he must be outside and by now probably very cross.

He was both outside and cross.

He was also Martland's man Maurice. (I suppose I hadn't really expected Martland to play it straight: the school we were at together wasn't a particularly good one. Long on sodomy and things but a bit short on the straight bat, honour and other expensive extras, although they talked a lot about them in Chapel. Cold baths a-plenty, of course, but you, who have never taken one, may be surprised to learn that your actual cold bath is your great begetter of your animal passions. Rotten bad for the heart, too, they tell me.)

Maurice had a newspaper in front of his face and was peering at me through a hole in it, just like they do in the storybooks. I took a couple of rapid paces to the left: the paper swung around after me. Then three to the right and again the paper swung, like the fire shield of a field gun. He did look silly. I walked over to him and poked my finger through the hole in his paper.

'Booh!' I said and waited for his devastating retort.

'Please take your finger out of my newspaper,' he retorted devastatingly.

I wiggled the finger, resting my nose on the top of the newspaper.

'Piss off!' he snarled, scarlet-faced. Better, that.

I pissed off, well pleased with myself. Round the corner of St

James's Street clumped a policeman, one of those young, pink, indignant policemen you meet so often nowadays. Ambitious, virtuous and hell on evil-doers.

'Officer!' I gobbled angrily, 'I have just been obscenely accosted by that wretched fellow with the newspaper.' I pointed a shaking finger at Maurice who paused guiltily in midstride. The policeman went white about the lips and bore down on Maurice who was still on one foot, newspaper outstretched, looking extraordinarily like a cruel parody of Gilbert's 'Eros' at Piccadilly Circus. (Did you know that Eros is made of aluminium? I'm sure there's a moral there somewhere. Or a joke.)

'I'll be at your Station in forty minutes,' I cried after the policeman, and nipped into a passing taxi. It had all its handles.

Now, as I've already told you, Martland's men have a year's training. Ergo, spotting Maurice so easily had to mean that Maurice was there to be spotted. It took me a long time but I spotted her in the end: a burly, clean-shaven, auntlike woman in a Triumph Herald: an excellent car for tailing people in, unremarkable, easily parked and with a tighter turning circle than a London taxi. It was unfair on her not to have had a companion though. I simply hopped out at Piccadilly Circus, went in one Underground entrance and out of another. Triumph Heralds are not all that easily parkable.

My second taxi took me to Bethnal Green Road, Shoreditch, a wonderful place where all sorts of recondite crafts are plied. Over-tipping the driver, as is my foolish wont, he 'gave' me 'Nostalgia for the fourth at Kempton Park.' Still wondering what on earth he could mean, I climbed the stairs to my liner's studio.

Here I'd better explain what a liner is. Most old paintings need a new support before they can be cleaned. In its simplest form, this involves soaking the old canvas with glue, 'compo' or wax, then bonding it, so to speak, to a new canvas by means of a hot table and pressure. Sometimes the old canvas is too far gone; sometimes during the work the paint comes adrift (the picture 'blows up' as they say). In either of these cases a 'transfer' is called for. This means that the painting is fastened face downwards and every shred of canvas is removed from the paint. The new canvas is then stuck onto the back of the paint and your picture is sound again. If it is painted on panel (wood) which has gone rotten or wormy, a really top reliner can plane all the wood off, leaving only the crust of paint, to which he then sticks a canvas. All very, very tricky work and highly paid. A good liner has a pretty shrewd idea of the value of the painting he is treating and usually charges accordingly. He makes more money than many of the dealers he works for. He is indispensable. Any idiot can clean a painting – and many of them do – and most competent artists can strengthen (touch up) or replace missing bits of paint; indeed many famous painters have made a good thing out of this as a secret sideline. (Very delicate work, like the rigging of ships, was often painted with a varnish medium for easy handling: this is hell to clean because, of course, it comes off with the dirty varnish. Consequently, many cleaners simply photograph the rigging or whatever, ruthlessly clean it off, then repaint it from the photograph. Well, why not?) But a good liner, as I was saying, is a pearl beyond price.

Pete does not look like a pearl. He looks like a dirty and sinister little Welshman, but he has the curiously beautiful manners which even the basest Celt displays in his own home. He opened the ceremonial tin of Spam and brewed a huge metal pot of lovely strong Brooke Bond PG Tips. I hastily volunteered to make the bread and butter – his nails were *filthy* – and to slice the Spam. It was a lovely tea party, I adore Spam, and the tea had condensed milk in it and came out a rich orange colour. (How different, how very different, from the home life of our own dear queen.)

I told him the Spränger would be arriving from Sotheby's and that I thought the drapery over Venus's oh-be-joyful was later work and probably concealed a very fair example of the nun's wink.

'Scrub,' I told him, 'but scrub with care.'

We then repaired to his studio under the roof so that I could inspect work in progress. All very satisfactory. He was having great trouble with my little Sienese tryptich (*is* that how you spell it?) but then he'd been having trouble with it for eighteen months. I never got the bill for it and now I probably never shall.

Then I told him about Mr Spinoza and explained certain new arrangements. He didn't like them a bit but soon stopped shrieking when

I filled his mouth with gold, as it were. He keeps his money in the tea caddy, if you want to know. There was one more ordeal to be undergone before I could get away from his carious, onion-laden breath.

'Just got time for a tune, then, ain't I?' he cried with the coy, treat-giving air of a Quartermaster dishing out prophylactics.

'Capital, capital,' I responded, rubbing hypocritical hands. He sat down at his little electric organ (it cost him £4oo) and treated me to 'Turn back, oh man, Forswear thy foolish ways' which moved me deeply. There is something curiously wrong about most Welsh voices, a kind of cardboard quality under the slick of gold, which irks me greatly. Pete's singing can reduce a public bar full of people to tears of sheer pleasure – I've seen it – but it always makes me feel that I've eaten too many Spam sandwiches.

I applauded loudly and, since he was particularly indispensable at that juncture, begged humbly for another. He gave me 'There is a Fountain Filled with Blood,' which never fails to please. I tottered downstairs and into the street, my bowels heavy with strong tea and foreboding.

The Bethnal Green Road at half past six on a Saturday night is not a *locus classicus* for taxis. In the end I took a bus; the conductor wore a turban and hated me on sight. I could see him memorizing me so that he could go on hating me after I'd got off.

Much depressed, I entered the flat and stood limply while Jock took my hat and coat away from me. He steered me to my favourite chair and brought me a glass of whisky calculated to stun a Clydesdale stallion. I revived enough to play a record of Amelita Galli-Curci singing 'Un Di Felice' with Tito Schipa; that reassured me in the *bel canto* department and the rest of the album dissipated most of the foreboding. Bathed and dinner-jacketed, I was in the mood for Wilton's lovely *art-nouveau* décor and even more in the mood for their Oysters Mornay. I also had a baked custard, a thing I wouldn't dream of eating anywhere else.

Home again, I was in time for a rattling John Wayne Western on the television, which I let Jock watch with me. We drank a great deal of whisky, for this was Saturday night.

I suppose I went to bed at some stage.

5

For he 'gins to guess the purpose of the garden,
With the sly mute thing beside, there, for a warden.

What's the leopard-dog-thing, constant at his side,
A leer and lie in every eye of its obsequious hide?

You must have noticed from time to time, self-indulgent reader, that
brandy, unless you positively stupefy yourself with it, tends to drive
sleep away, rather than induce it. I am told, by those who have drunk it,
that with cheap brandy the effect is even more marked. It is otherwise
with Scotch whisky; a benign fluid. All credit, I say, to the man who
first invented it, be his skin of whatever hue. Indeed, my only quarrel
with him is that sixteen fluid ozs of his brainchild, taken orally *per
diem* for ten years or so, lessens one's zest for the primal act. I used
to think that my flagging powers were the result of advancing age
combining with the ennui natural to an experienced *coureur*, but Jock
disabused me. He calls it 'brewer's droop'.

Be that as it may, I find that drinking a sound twelve-year-old
Scotch in good quantity gives me six hours of flawless slumber, followed by a compulsion to get up in the morning and bustle about.
Accordingly, I got up, without the sweet coercion of Bohea, and
stamped downstairs, intending to roust Jock out and point out to him
the benefits of early rising. To my mild chagrin he was already up and
out of the flat, so I made my own breakfast: a bottle of Bass. I can
heartily recommend it. I shall not pretend that I would not have liked
a cup of tea, but the truth is that I am a little afraid of these new electric kettles: in my experience they eject their plugs savagely at you
while you stand beside them waiting for them to boil.

There is only one thing to do early on a Sunday morning in London and that is to visit Club Row. I tiptoed downstairs so as not to disturb my Madame Defarge and made my way to the mews. All three cars were there but Jock's huge motorbike, which generates enough power to light a small town, was absent. I gave a whimsical Gallic wink and shrug to a passing cat: Jock was probably in love again, I thought. When chaps like him are in rut they'll travel miles, you know, escaping from prison first if needs be.

Club Row used to be just a row of shifty chaps selling stolen dogs: nowadays it is an enormous open-air mart. I roved about for an hour but the old magic didn't work. I bought a disgusting plastic object to tease Jock with – it was called 'Drat That Dog' – and drove home, too distraught even to lose my way. I thought of dropping in at Farm Street to catch one of those rattling Jesuit sermons but felt that might be too dangerous in my present mood. The sweet logic and lucidity of high-powered Jesuits works on me like a siren-song and I have a dread that one day I shall be Saved – like a menopausal woman – *how* Mrs Spon would laugh! Do they really wash you in the blood of the lamb or is that only the Salvation Army?

Jock was at home, elaborately unsurprised at my early rising. We did not question each other. While he cooked my breakfast I slipped the 'Drat That Dog' into the canary's cage.

Then I had a little zizz until Martland telephoned.

'Look, Charlie,' he quacked, 'it just isn't on. I can't organize all that Diplomatic bit, the Foreign Office told me to go and piss up my kilt.'

I was in no mood to be trifled with by the Martlands of this world.

'Very well,' I rapped out crisply, 'let us forget the whole thing.' And I hung up. Then I changed my clothes and laid a course for the Café Royal and luncheon.

'Jock,' I said as I left, 'Mr Martland will be telephoning again shortly to say that everything is all right after all. Tell him "all right," would you. All right?'

'All right, Mr Charlie.'

The Café Royal was full of people pretending they went there often. I liked my lunch but I forget what it was.

When I got back to the flat Jock told me that Martland had called in person, all the way from what he calls Canonbury, to wrangle with me, but that Jock had turned him away.

'He bloody near spit on the mat' was how Jock summed up his parting mood.

I went to bed and read a naughty book until I fell asleep, which was soon. You can't get good naughty books any more, there aren't the craftsmen nowadays, you see. Those Swedish ones with coloured photographs are the worst, don't you think? Like illustrations to a handbook of gynaecology.

Mrs Spon woke me up, charging into my bedroom in a red, wet-look trouser suit; she looked like a washable Scarlet Woman. I hid under the bedclothes until she promised she was only here to play Gin Rummy. She plays a lovely game of Gin but has terrible luck, poor dear; I usually win six or seven pounds off her but then she's had a fortune from me at interior decorating. (It is my invariable practice, when playing Gin Rummy, to leave one card accidentally in the box: it is amazing how much edge you can get from the knowledge that there is, for example, no nine of spades in the pack.)

After a while she complained of the cold as she always does – I will not have central heating, it ruins one's antique furniture and dries up one's tubes. So she got into bed beside me, as she always does (look, she must be sixty for God's sake), and we played 'gotcha' for a while between hands. Then she rang for Jock who brought a naked sword to put between us and a lot of hot pastrami sandwiches on garlicky bread. We were drinking Valpolicella, hell on the bowels but delicious and so cheap. I won six or seven pounds from her; it was such a lovely evening; tears start to my eyes as I recall it. It is no use treasuring these moments as they occur, it spoils them; they are only for remembering.

When she had gone, after one last 'gotcha', Jock brought me my bedtime rations: whisky, milk, chicken sandwiches and aluminium hydroxide for the ulcer.

'Jock,' I said, after thanking him civilly, 'we must do something about nasty Perce, Mr O'Flaherty's little git.'

'I already done it, Mr Charlie. 'Smorning, before you was up.'

'Did you really, Jock? My word, you think of everything. Did you hurt him very much?'

'Yes, Mr Charlie.'

'Oh dear. Not.'

'Nah. Nuffing that a good dentist couldn't put right in a coupla munce. And, uh, I don't reckon he'll feel like doing any *courting* for a bit, either, see what I mean.'

'Poor little chap,' I said.

'Yeah,' said Jock. 'Goodnight, Mr Charlie.'

'One other thing,' I said crisply. 'I am disturbed at the state of hygiene in the canary's cage. Could you see that it's cleaned out soon, please?'

'I already done it, Mr Charlie. While you was out at lunch.'

'Oh. Everything all right?'

'Yeah. 'Course.'

'Oh, well, thanks, Jock. Goodnight.'

I didn't sleep very well that night.

If either Krampf or Gloag had departed from the agreed plan I could have borne it with fortitude, but two idiots in a team of three seemed excessive. I had told Hockbottle Gloag when he first approached me that I had no intention of helping him to blackmail his august Chum – introducing Hockers to Krampf was as far as I was prepared to go. Later, when Krampf had suggested to me that the photograph could be used, not for coarse money squeezing, but for facilitating the export, to him, of hot works of art, I had let him wring from me my slow consent, but only on condition that I should write the script, and play both the lead and the comic relief. But, as Schnozzle Durante never tired of saying, 'Everybody wants to get in on the act.' Gloag had already paid the price for this foot-light fever and it looked as though Krampf was at least getting a pro forma invoice.

6

Still, what if I approach the august sphere
Named now with only one name, disentwine
That under-current soft and argentine
From its fierce mate . . .?

Sordello

The telephone woke me at a most *inconvenient* hour on Monday. A honeyed American voice asked if it could speak to Mr Mortdecai's secretary.

'One moooment please,' I crooned, 'I'll put you throooo.' I stuffed the telephone under my pillow and lit a cigarette, musing the while. Finally I rang for Jock, briefed him and gave him the telephone. Holding it between hairy thumb and forefinger, pinky delicately crooked, he fluted, 'Mr Mortdecai's seckritry 'ere.' Then he got the giggles – disastrous after yesterday's feast of beans – and so did I and the telephone got dropped; the Honeyed American Voice must have thought it all *most* peculiar. It turned out that it – the H.A.V. – was a Colonel Blucher's secretary at the American Embassy, and that Colonel Blucher would like to see Mr Mortdecai at ten o'clock. Jock, properly shocked, said that there was no chance of Mr Mortdecai being out of bed at that hour and that he never received gentlemen in bed. (More giggles.) The voice, no whit less honeyed, said that, well, Colonel Blucher had in fact envisaged Mr. Mortdecai calling on *him* and would ten thirty be more convenient. Jock fought a stout rear-guard action – in a curious way he's rather proud to work for anyone as slothful as me – and finally they struck a bargain for noon.

As soon as Jock put the instrument down I lifted it again and dialed the Embassy (499 9000, if you want to know). One of the most beautiful voices I have ever heard answered – a furry, milky contralto which made my coccyx curl into ringlets. It quite distinctly said:

'Care to embrace me?'

'Eh?' I gobbled, 'what's that what's that?'

'American Embassy' – this time in rather more sanitary tones.

'Oh. Yes. Of course. Silly of me. Ah, what I wanted to know was whether you have a Colonel Blucher working there.'

There was a click or two, a muted electric 'grrr' and before I could do anything about it I was once more in communication with the original Honeyed (honied?) Voice. She didn't say she was Colonel anyone's secretary this time, she said she was the War Room, CumQuicJac or SecSatSix or some such mumbo-jumbo. What *children* these warriors are.

I couldn't very well say that I was just checking to see whether Col. Blucher was real or just a Heartless Practical Joke, could I? In the end, after a bit of spluttering, I said that I had an appointment with her guv'nor, d'ye see, at sort of noon really, and what number in Grosvenor Square was the Embassy. This should have been a heavy score to me – lovely footwork you must admit – but she was a fast, damaging counterpuncher.

'Number twenty-four,' she warbled unhesitatingly, 'that's two, four.'

I rang off after a mumbled civility or two. Rolled up, horse, foot and guns. I mean, fancy a bloody great place like that having a street number, for God's sake.

Jock averted his gaze: he knows when the young master has taken a bit of stick.

I pushed my breakfast moodily round the plate for a while then told Jock to give it to the deserving poor and bring me in its stead a large glass of gin with both sorts of vermouth in it and some fizzy lemonade. A quick actor, that drink, gets you to where you live in no time.

Sucking a perfumed cachou, I walked to Grosvenor Square, soberly clad and musing madly. The musing was to no avail; my mind was as blank as the new, soft fallen mask of snow upon the mountains and the moors. The cachou lasted as far as the portals of the Embassy, within which stood a capable-looking military man, standing at what is laughingly called ease. The jut of his craggy jaw made it clear to the trained eye that he was there to keep out Commie bastards and anyone else who might be plotting to overthrow the Constitution of the United States. I met his eye fearlessly and asked him if this was number twenty-four and he didn't know, which made me feel better.

A succession of well-designed young ladies took charge of me, wafting me ever deeper into the building. Each one of them was tall, slim, hygienic, graceful and endowed with amazingly large tits: I'm afraid I probably stared rather. I fetched up all standing (nautical term) at the outer office of Col. Blucher, where sat the Voice itself. She, as was fitting, had the finest endowment of all. I should think she had to type at arm's length. In the twinkling of an eye – and I mean that most sincerely – I was shunted into the inner office, where a lean, wholesome, uniformed youth gave me a chair.

I recognized the chair as soon as I applied my bottom to it. It was covered with shiny leather and the front legs were half an inch shorter than the back legs. This gives the sitter a vague feeling of unease, impermanence, inferiority. I have one myself, for seating chaps on who are trying to sell paintings to me. On no account was I going to take crap of this kind; I arose and made for the sofa.

'Forgive me,' I said sheepishly, 'I have these piles, you know? Haemorrhoids?'

He knew. Judging from the smile he cranked on to his face, I should say he had just developed them. He sat down behind the desk. I raised an eyebrow.

'I have an appointment with Colonel Blucher,' I said.

'I am Colonel Blucher, sir,' replied the youth.

I'd lost that rally, anyway, but I was still ahead on the chair-to-sofa move, he had to twist his neck and raise his voice when he spoke to me. He looked extraordinarily young to be a colonel and, curiously, his uniform didn't fit. Have you ever seen an American officer – nay, an American *private* even – with an ill-fitting uniform?

Tucking this thought away into a mental ticket pocket, I addressed the man.

'Oh, ah,' was the phrase I selected.

Perhaps I could have done better, given more time.

He picked up a pen and teased a folder which lay on his shining, empty desk. The folder had all sorts of coloured signals stuck on to it, including a big orange-coloured one with an exclamation mark in black. I had a nasty feeling that perhaps the file was labelled 'Hon C Mortdecai' but on second thoughts I decided that it was just there to frighten me.

'Mr Mortdecai,' he said at last, 'we have been asked by your Foreign Office to honour a diplomatic *laissez-passer* in your name and on a temporary basis. There seems to be no intention to accredit you to the British Embassy in Washington or to any Legation or Consulate, and our *vis-à-vis* in your Foreign Office seems to know nothing about you. I may say we have received the impression that he cares less. Would you perhaps like to comment on this situation?'

'Nope,' I replied.

This seemed to please him. He changed to another pen and stirred the folder about a bit more.

'Mr Mortdecai, you will appreciate that I have to enter in my report the purpose of your visit to the United States.'

'I am to deliver a valuable antique motor car under diplomatic seal,' I said, 'and I hope to do a little sightseeing in the South and West. I am very interested in the Old West,' I added defiantly, smugly conscious of a card up my sleeve.

'Yes, indeed,' he said politely, 'I read your article on "Nineteenth Century British Travellers to the American Frontier." It was very very fascinating.'

There was a distinct draft up my sleeve where the card had been, and a nasty feeling that someone had been doing a little research into C. Mortdecai.

'We are puzzled,' he went on, 'that anyone should want to seal diplomatically an empty automobile. I take it that it will, in fact, be empty, Mr Mortdecai?'

'It will contain my personal effects; viz., one case of gents' natty suitings, one ditto of costly haberdashery, a canvas bag of books to suit every mood – none of them very obscene – and a supply of cigarettes and old Scotch whisky. I shall be happy to pay duty on the last if you prefer.'

'Mr Mortdecai, if we accept your diplomatic status' – did he linger a moment at that point? – 'we shall of course respect it fully. But we have, as you know, this theoretical right to declare you *persona non grata*; although we exercise it very rarely toward representatives of your country.'

'Yes,' I babbled, 'old Guy slipped through all right, didn't he?'

He pricked his ears; I bit my tongue.

'Did you know Mr Burgess well?' he asked, inspecting his pen closely for defects in its manufacture.

'No no no,' I cried, 'no no no no no. Hardly ever met the feller. Probably had a jar of sherbet with him once in a while: I mean, you couldn't live in the same city with Guy Burgess and not find yourself in the same bar sometimes, could you? Matter of statistics, I mean.'

He opened the folder and read a few lines, raising one eyebrow in a disturbing way.

'Have you ever been a member of the Communist or Anarchist parties, Mr Mortdecai?'

'Good Lord no!' I cried gaily, 'filthy capitalist, me. Grind the workers' faces, I say.'

'When you were at school?' he prompted gently.

'Oh. Well, yes, I think I did take the Red side in the debating society at school once or twice. But in the Lower Sixth we all got either religion or Communism – it goes with acne you know. Vanishes as soon as you have proper sexual intercourse.'

'Yes,' he said quietly. I suddenly saw that he had acne. Strike two, as I believe they say over there. And how on earth had they dredged up all this dirt about me in a couple of days? A more unnerving thought: *had* it only been dredged in the last couple of days? The folder looked fat and well-handled as a Welsh barmaid. I wanted to go to the lavatory.

The silence went on and on. I lit a cigarette to show how unperturbed I was but he was ready for that one, too. He pressed a button and told his secretary to ask the janitor for an ashtray. When she brought it she turned the air conditioner up as well. Strike three. My turn to pitch.

'Colonel,' I said crisply, 'suppose I give you my word of honour as a nobleman' – *that* was a spitball – 'that I am totally uninterested in politics and that my mission has nothing to do with drugs, contraband, currency, white slavery, perversion or the Mafia, but that it does concern the interests of some of the Highest in the Land?'

To my amazement it seemed to work. He nodded slowly, initialled the front of the file and sat back in his chair. Americans have some curious pockets of old-fashionedness. One could feel the atmosphere of the room relaxing; even the air conditioner seemed to have changed its note. I cocked an ear.

'Forgive me,' I said, 'but I think that your wire recorder has run out of wire.'

'Why, thank you,' he said and pressed another button. The mammiferous secretary slithered in, changed the spool and slithered out again, giving me a small, hygienic smile en route. An English secretary would have sniffed.

'Do you know Milton Krampf well?' Blucher asked suddenly. Clearly, the ball game was still on.

'Krampf?' I said. 'Krampf? Yes, to be sure, very good customer of mine. Hope to spend a few days with him. Very nice old sausage. Bit potty of course but he can afford to be, can't he, ha ha.'

'Well, no, Mr Mortdecai, I in fact was referring to Dr Milton Krampf III, Mr Milton Krampf Junior's son.'

'Ah, there you have me,' I said truthfully, 'never met any of the family.'

'Really, Mr Mortdecai? Yet Dr Krampf is a well-known art historian, is he not?'

'News to me. What's his field supposed to be?' The Colonel flipped through the file – perhaps it was the *Krampf* file after all.

'He seems to have published numerous papers in American and Canadian journals,' he said, 'including "The Non-Image in Dérain's Middle Period," "Chromato-Spacial Relationships in Dufy," "Léger and Counter-Symbolism". . .'

'Stop!' I cried, squirming. 'Enough. I could make up the rest of the titles myself. I know this sort of thing well, it has nothing to do with art history as I know it; my work lies with the Old Masters and I publish in the *Burlington Magazine* – I am quite a different sort of snob from this Krampf, our scholarly paths would never cross.'

'I see.'

He didn't see at all but he would have died rather than admit it. We parted in the usual flurry of insincerities. He still looked young, but not quite as young as when I had come in. I walked home, musing again.

Jock had a sauté of chicken livers ready for me but I had no stomach for the feast. Instead I chewed a banana and about a third of a bottle of gin. Then I had a little zizz, a little slumber, a little folding of the hands in sleep. A zizz, you know, is a very present help in trouble. With me, it takes the place of the kind, wise, tobacco-smelling, tweed-clad *English* father that other boys had when I was a schoolboy; the sort of father you could talk things over with during long tramps over the hills; who would gruffly tell you that 'a chap can only do his best' and that you 'must play the man' and then teach you to cast a trout-fly.

My father wasn't like that.

Sleep has often taken the place of this mythical man for me: often I have woken up comforted and advised, my worries resolved, my duty clear.

But this time I awoke unrefreshed and with no good news teeming in my brain. There was no comfortable feeling that a warm, tweedy arm had been about my shoulder, only the old gin-ache at the base of the skull and a vague taste of dog dung in the mouth.

'Heigh-ho,' I remember saying as I listened to the Alka-Seltzer fussing in its glass. I tried the effect of a clean shirt and a washed face; there was some slight improvement but various small nit-sized worries were still there. I have a dislike for coincidences and I detest clever young American colonels, especially when their uniforms do not quite fit them.

I was rather a cheery, carefree chap in those days, always ready to welcome a little adversity just for the pleasure of dealing with it deftly. So I was worried at feeling worried, if you see what I mean.

One should only have a sense of impending doom when one is constipated and I was not, as it happened.

Jock handed me a stiff envelope when I emerged: it had been delivered, while I slept, by what he described as a long streak of pee in a bowler hat. Jock, with unerring aim, had offered him a pint of beer in the kitchen, which had been refused with some brusqueness.

The writer, who seemed to be assistant private secretary to someone else's permanent under-secretary or something, said that he was instructed to request me (or was it the other way about? – I forget) to present myself at Room 504 in one of the uglier new Government office blocks at 10.30 a.m. the following day, there to meet a Mr L.J. Crouch.

Now, I have only two basic rules for the conduct of my life, to wit:

Rule A My time and services are at the complete disposal of the customer at any time of the day or night and no trouble is too great when the interests of others can be served.

Rule B On the other hand, I'm buggered if I'm going to be buggered about.

I handed the note to Jock.

'This clearly falls under Rule B, does it not, Jock?'

'Dead right it does, Mr Charlie.'

'Ten thirty is the time stated?'

'Yeah.'

'Then call me at eleven in the morning.'

'O.K., Mr Charlie.'

Happier after that expression of poco-curantism, I strolled down to Veersawamy's and thoughtfully gorged myself with curried lamb and buttered chapatis. The splendidly dressed doorman gave me his usual splendidly military salute in exchange for the shiniest half crown I could find in my pocket. Cheap at the price. When depressed, go and find someone to salute you.

Curry, in my small experience, makes women want to go to bed and make love; it just makes me want to go to bed and get the weight off my stomach. Curiously ponderous stuff, curry.

I carried my freight distressfully to bed and Jock brought me whisky and soda to cool the blood. I read Karl Popper's *Poverty of*

Historicism for a while then fell asleep to dream guilty, furtive dreams about Punjabi colonels in deerstalker hats.

The burglar alarm went off at 3 a.m. When we are at home this only takes the form of a low, whining noise, pitched at a menacing frequency, which sounds in both bedrooms, both bathrooms, the drawing room and Jock's bog. It stops as soon as each of us has pressed a switch, so that we know we are both alert. I pressed my switch and it stopped immediately. I went to my post, which is an armchair in the darkest corner of my bedroom, after I had stuffed my bolster under the covers to simulate a sleeping Mortdecai. Above the armchair is a trophy of antique firearms, one of which is an 8-bore shotgun by Joe Manton, loaded with dust shot in the right-hand barrel, BB in the other. An old-fashioned bell pull below it releases the clamps which hold it to the wall. My job was to lurk there motionless, watching the door and the windows. Jock, meantime, would have checked the bellboard to ascertain where the alarm had been triggered from, then stationed himself by the tradesmen's door whence he could cut off retreats and, if necessary, follow an intruder upstairs to my room. I lurked, in a deadly silence broken only by my load of curry, which was churning about inside me like socks in a washing machine. It is very difficult to be frightened when you are gripping a loaded 8-bore shotgun but I managed it. This should not have been *happening*, you see.

After an eon or two the alarm made one brief peep, which was my signal to go downstairs. Sodden with funk, I crept down to the kitchen, where Jock stood naked and shadowy by the door, balancing an old 9-mm Luger in his hand. On the bellboard a violet light marked FRONT DOOR was still flickering frantically. With a couple of jerks of the head Jock outlined our tactics: I slid into the drawing room where I could cover lobby and front door, Jock silently drew the bolts of the tradesmen's door. I heard him wrench it open and bound into the corridor – then he called me low and urgently. I ran through the dining room, into the kitchen, out of the door. Only Jock was in the corridor. I followed his stare to the lift indicator: it said '5' – my floor. At that moment the lift motor growled and the '5' flicked out and Jock hurtled to the stairhead and vanished downwards with scarcely a sound. You should have seen Jock in action – an intimidating sight, especially when naked, as then. I ran down half a flight until I could see into the well of the staircase: Jock had taken up a position on the ground floor, covering the lift doors. After a second or two he jumped up and vanished into the back regions; puzzled for a moment, I suddenly realized that the lift must have gone down into the basement. I galloped down, humpetty-dump, all fright forgotten now, and had reached the third floor when a glance at the indicator showed me that the lift was again rising. Up I fled again, arriving at the fifth floor sadly blown. The indicator had stopped at '3'. I slammed into the flat, stumbled through into the drawing room and knelt down beside the record-player console. A button inside it communicated with the 'Set-A-Thief' duty room – I yearned for those thugs. I didn't press the button, for someone hit me at the base of the skull, just where my gin-ache still lingered. My chin hooked on to the edge of the console and there I hung awhile, feeling very silly. Then he hit me again and I sank effortlessly through the floor, miles and miles and miles.

About a lifetime later I awoke, with great reluctance. Jock's huge face hung moonlike over me, making worried noises. When I spoke, shattering echoes boomed and rattled through my poor head. I was filled with hatred and misery.

'Did you kill him?' I asked hungrily.

'No, Mr Charlie. I waited at the bottom for a bit and the lift stopped at "3" and I waited a bit more then I tried the button and it came down empty so I went up in it to here and you weren't outside so I went to the top of the stairs to see if I could see you and then I heard the lift going down again and I thought this could go on all bleeding night and I came in here looking for you and here you were and so I thought . . .' I raised a hand feebly.

'Stop,' I said. 'I cannot possibly follow all this at the moment. It makes my head hurt. Search the flat, lock the doors, get me to bed and find me the largest sleeping pill ever made. And get some clothes on, you idiot, you'll catch your death.'

At this point I switched off C. Mortdecai as an individual and let the poor chap swim through the floor again, down to a sunless sea.

If anyone cut my throat after that, they were welcome.

7

Who'd stoop to blame
This sort of trifling? Even had you skill
In speech (which I have not) – to make your will
Quite clear to such an one, and say, 'Just this
Or that in you disgusts me; here you miss,
Or there exceed the mark' – . . .
– E'en then would be some stooping; and I choose
Never to stoop.

My Last Duchess

I very carefully levered up an eyelid and shut it again fast. A merciless sunbeam had squirted straight in, making my brain bleed.

Much later I tried again.

The sunshine had been smothered and Jock was hovering at the foot of my bed, wringing his hands. He was also carrying a tea tray, but I have the distinct impression that he was wringing the hands, too.

'Go away,' I whimpered. He set the tray down and poured a cup for me; it sounded, inside my poor head, like someone flushing a lavatory in an echo chamber. I whimpered a little more and turned away but Jock gently waggled my shoulder, murmuring, 'Now now' or 'There there' or words to that effect. I sat up to remonstrate with him – the action seemed to leave half my skull behind on the pillow. I felt the afflicted area gingerly: it was sort of spongy and squashy to the touch but to my surprise was not caked with blood. I decided that had my skull been fractured I would not have woken up at all. Not that it seemed to matter that morning.

The tea was not my customary Lapsang or Oolong but Twining's robuster Queen Mary's Blend: shrewd Jock, he knew that a morning like this called for sterner stuff. I got the first cupful down, then Jock fed me two Alka-Seltzers (the *noise!*), two Beecham's Powders and two dexedrines, in the order named, washing the whole collection down with a second cup of Queen Mary's best and brightest. I shall never say another harsh word about that sainted woman.

Soon I became capable once more of rational thought, and rational thought urged me to go back to sleep at once. I sank down in the general direction of the pillows but Jock firmly scooped me up and balanced cups of tea all over me so that I dared not move.

'There's this tart been ringing up all day,' he said, 'says she's that deputy secretary bloke's secretary and it's about your travel papers and you ought to get around there if you can stand and her gaffer'll see you any time up to half past four. It's three now, nearly.'

Creaking and grunting I hoisted myself to the surface.

'Who do you think it was then last night, Mr Charlie?'

'Not one of Martland's lot, anyway,' I answered. 'They would have expected the full treatment like last time. Anything missing?'

'Not that I can see.'

'Well, they didn't go to all that trouble just to sock me on the back of the head, that's for certain.'

'Could have just been an ordinary villain: hadn't cased us proper, didn't reckon on two of us, lost his head and buggered off a bit sharpish. He left this stuck in the front door lock, that's why the alarm light kept on.'

'This' was a pocket calendar made of stiff celluloid, the size and shape of a playing card, bearing on the reverse an impassioned plea for the reader to drink someone's Milk Stout. It would diddle open almost any sort of spring cylinder lock. It would be useless against my Chubb dead-lock with the phosphor-bronze rollers in the wards, and anyone who had spent even a week's remedial training in Borstal would have known that. I didn't like it. Raw novices do not try their prentice hands on fifth floor penthouse flats in Upper Brook Street.

I started to think about it for the first time and liked it less and less.

'Jock,' I said, 'if we disturbed him while he was trying to celly the lock, why wasn't he *there* when we disturbed him? And since he wasn't *there*, how could he discover there were two of us? And if he'd given it up *before* you popped out, why did he leave a useful celly behind and why did he linger in the lift instead of, ah, buggering off a bit sharpish?'

Jock opened his mouth a bit to help him think. I could see that it hurt him.

'Never mind,' I said, kindly, 'I know how you feel. Mine hurts too. It seems to me that the villain poked his celly into the lock just to trigger the alarm, then lay in wait in the lift. When you popped out, he popped down, to draw you away. Then up again to the third, knowing you would wait for him downstairs like a sensible chap; out of the lift and up to the fifth on foot, knowing that he could handle me alone. Having done so, he hears you arrive, hides behind a door and exits quietly while you are succouring the young master. The whole idea was to get me alone with the door open and you safely out of the way for a few minutes. What we need to wonder is not how, or even who, but why.'

'Taking something . . .'

'If so, it must have been something portable, easily found – because he can't have expected much time – and something very important to make the risk worthwhile. Something recently arrived, too, probably, because there is a sort of impromptu aroma about the whole thing.'

'. . . or leaving something,' Jock continued with remorseless logic.

I jumped, making my headache rear up and smite me. It was a nasty thought, that one.

'What on earth would anyone want to leave here?' I squeaked, dreading the answer.

'Well, like a bug,' said Jock. 'Or a couple of ounces of heroin, enough to put you inside for twelve munce. Or say arf a pound of plastic explosive . . .'

'I am going back to bed,' I said firmly. 'I want no part of any of this. Nobody ordered bombs.'

'No, Mr Charlie, you got to go to this assistant secretary geezer. I'll nip round to the garage and fetch the big jam jar.'

'What, and leave me alone in a flat *sown* with Teller mines?' I wailed.

But he was gone. Grumbling bitterly I climbed into a random

assortment of gents' wear and crept through the flat and downstairs. Nothing exploded under my feet.

Jock was awaiting me at street level in the Rolls and as a special treat for me he was wearing his chauffeur's cap. When we arrived at the Ministry he even jumped out and opened the door for me; he knew it would cheer me up, bless him.

Do you know, I honestly can't remember which Ministry it was; this was soon after the Wilson administration, you see, and you remember how he muddled them all up and changed all the names. They say that there are still a few lorn civil servants haunting the pavements of Whitehall like ghosts, plucking at strangers' sleeves and begging to be told the way to the Ministry of Technological Integration. Their salaries keep on coming, of course, because of Giro, but what really hurts them most is that their Ministries haven't *missed* them yet.

Be that as it may, Jock left me at this Ministry and various super young men passed me through door after door – each young man more beautifully dressed, each door heavier and silenter than the last – until I was alone with L.J. Crouch. I had fortified myself against a sort of English Colonel Blucher but nothing could have been further from the facts. A great, jolly, big-boned, straw-haired chap lowered his boots from a well-chewed desk and lumbered to meet me, beaming merrily.

'Ha!' he roared, 'Capital! Glad to see you on your feet, young feller! Best thing after a crunch – get up and charge about. *Nil illegitimis carborundum*, eh? Don't let the bastards wear you down!'

I tittered feebly and sank into the fat leather armchair he indicated. Cigars, whisky and soda were conjured into my listless hands while I gazed around me. The furniture, unmistakably, came from a better class vicarage: all well made but sort of trodden on. In front of me, above his chair, sixty rat-faced boys squinted and goggled at me from a prep school group photograph; above them hung a piece of an Eights oar, splintered and charred and bearing the colours of St. Edmund Hall. In a corner sat an old brass naval shell-case, crammed with stout sticks and fencing foils of the old butterfly-hilted *fleuret* pattern. Two walls were hung with early English watercolours of the

good, drab, bluish kind. Nothing is more tedious, as Sir Karl Parker
used to say, than an early English watercolour – unless it be a *faded*
early English watercolour. But I cut my business teeth on them and
always hold them in respect.

'Know about watercolours?' asked Crouch, following my gaze.

'A bit,' I said, looking him straight in the eye. 'You have a J. M.
W. Turner of the Loire which can't be right because the original is in
the Ashmolean; a magnificent Callow of about 1840; a Farington
which needs cleaning; a polychrome James Bourne – rare, those; a
Peter de Wint hayfield with a repainted sky; an excellent John Sell
Cotman; a pair of rather flashy Varleys from his last period; a Payne
which was reproduced in *Connoisseur* before the war; a Rowlandson
which Sabine had for sale in about 1940; a Francis Nicholson of
Scarborough all faded pink – he would use indigo; a valuable Cozens
and the finest Edridge I have ever seen.'

'My word' he said. 'Full marks, Mortdecai. I see you know about
watercolours.'

'Can't resist showing off,' I said sheepishly. 'Just a knack, really.'

'Mind you, the Edridge was sold me as a Girtin.'

'They always are,' I said simply.

'Well, come on, what'll you give me for the lot?'

A dealer has to get used to this sort of thing. I used to take offence
once upon a time, before I learned the value of money.

'Two thousand, two hundred and fifty,' I said, still looking him
straight in the eye. He was startled.

'*Pounds?*'

'Guineas,' I replied. 'Naturally.'

'God bless my soul. I stopped buying years ago, when the dear old
Walker Galleries closed. I knew prices had gone up but . . .'

'The prices of these will be going down unless you get them out of
this sunny room. They've taken about as much fading as they'll
stand.'

Ten minutes later he took my cheque with trembling fingers. I let
him keep the Nicholson in exchange for an Albert Goodwin which
had been hanging in the cloakroom. His outer door opened a fraction
and closed again with a respectful click. He started like a guilty thing

and looked at the clock. It was 4.30: he was going to miss his train. So were his beautiful young men, if he didn't look sharp.

'Repeat after me,' he said briskly, pulling a grubby piece of card from a desk drawer, 'I, Charlie Strafford Van Cleef Mortdecai, a true and loyal servant of Her Britannic Majesty, do solemnly swear . . .'

I gaped at the man. Was he doubting my cheque?

'Come on,' he said, 'cough it up, old chap.'

I coughed it up, line by line, swearing to be a faithful carrier of Her Majesty's messages within and without her realms notwithstanding, heretofore, whatsoever and so help me God. Then he gave me a little jeweller's box with a rummy-looking silver dog inside, a document starting 'We, Barbara Castle, request and require' and a thin, red leather folder stamped in gold with the words 'Court of St. James's.' I signed things until my hand ached.

'Don't know what it's all about and don't want to,' he kept saying as I signed. I respected his wishes.

The young men shunted me out, glaring at me for making them miss their trains. Creatures of habit, of course. Couldn't stand the life myself.

Martland was parked on a double yellow line outside, pulling rank on a brace of traffic wardens; in another moment he would have been telling them to get their hair cut. He waved me crossly into his awful basketwork Mini and took me to the American Embassy, where a mild, bored man spattered my new papers with State Department seals and wished me a vurry, vurry happy visit to the US of A. Then back to the flat, where I gave Martland a drink and he gave me a wallet-load of airline tickets, freight vouchers and the like, also a typed list of timetables, names and procedures. (Codswallop, all of it, that last lot.) He was silent, sulky preoccupied. He said it wasn't he that had had me turned over the night before, and he didn't much care who had. On the other hand he didn't seem particularly surprised: more vexed, really. I suspected that he was beginning to suspect, with me, that the tangled web we weave was starting to get our knickers in a twist. Like me, he may have been wondering who, after all, was manipulating whom.

'Charlie,' he said ponderously, his hand on the door knob, 'if you are by any chance conning me over that Goya picture, or if you let me down over this Krampf matter, I shall have to have you done, you realize that, don't you? In fact I may have to do it anyway.'

I invited him to feel the back of my head, which felt like a goitre which had lost its sense of direction, but he refused in an offensive way. He slammed the door when he went out and my cosh-ache reverberated.

8

. . . Bearing aloft another Ganymede
On pinions imped, as 't were, but not past bearing,
Nor unfit yet for the fowler's purposes;
Feathered, in short, as a prince o' th'air – no moorgame.
If Paracelsus weighs that jot, this tittle,
God knows your atomy were ponderable –
(Love weighing t'other pan down!) . . .
. . . in a word,
In half a word's space, – let's say, ere you flinched,
Or Paracelsus wove one of those thoughts,
Lighter than lad's-love, delicate as death,
I'd draft you thither.

Paracelsus

I was off to the Americas – it was the first day of the hols. I sprang out
of bed, calling for my bucket and spade, my sandshoes and my sun hat.
Without the aid of stimulants I gambolled downstairs, carolling –

> 'This time tomorrow I shall be
> Far from this Academee,'

disturbing Jock who was moodily packing my lightweights for the
American adventure.

'You all right, Mr Charlie?' he asked nastily.

'Jock, I cannot tell you how all right I am –

> "No more Latin, no more French,
> No more sitting on the hard school bench,"'

I went on.

It was a fine morning which would have earned *proxime accessit*
from Pippa herself. The sun was shining, the canary bellowing with

joy. Breakfast was cold kedgeree of which I ate great store – nothing nicer – washed down with bottled beer. Jock was sulking a little at being left behind but was really looking forward to having the flat to himself; he has his friends in to play dominoes when I'm away, I believe.

Then I opened about a week's accumulated mail, made out a pay-ing-in slip, wrote a few cheques for the more importunate creditors, telephoned Dial-A-Dolly and dictated a dozen letters, had lunch.

Before setting out on a lengthy expedition I always have the same lunch which Ratty made for the Sea Rat and which they ate on the grass by the roadside. Ratty, you will remember, *literate* reader, '. . . packed a simple meal in which . . . , he took care to include a yard of long French bread, a sausage out of which the garlic sang, some cheese which lay down and cried, and a long-necked straw-covered flask containing bottled sunshine and garnered on far Southern slopes.'

I pity anyone whose saliva does not flow in sympathy with those beautiful lines. How many men of my age have tastes and appetites distantly governed by these – not even half-remembered – words?

Jock drove me to Mr Spinoza's where we loaded the Silver Ghost with my suitcases (one pigskin, one canvas), and the book bag. Spinoza's foreman, with almost Japanese good taste, had not ham-mered out the bullet dimple in the door but had drilled it out and inlaid a disc of burnished brass, neatly engraved with Spinoza's ini-tials and the date on which he had gone to meet his jealous god – 'the Maker of the makers of all makes' as Kipling has so deftly put it.

Spinoza and I had had some difficulty in dissuading Krampf from having a synchro-mesh gear-box fitted to the Ghost; now every sprocket and shaft in it was a perfect replica of the original contents of the box, with thirty thousand miles of simulated wear lovingly buffed in by the naughty apprentice. The gears engaged in a way which reminded me of a warm spoon going in to a great deal of caviar. The foreman's metaphor was perhaps more general than caviar – he likened it to having hasty congress with a lady of easy virtue whom he was in the habit of patronizing. I stared at the fellow: he was nearly twice my age.

'I admire you,' I cried, admiringly. 'However do you manage to keep so virile in the evening of your days?'

'Ah, well, Sir,' he replied modestly, 'your verality is a matter of your actual birth and breeding. My farver was a terrible man for rumpy-pumpy; he had hair thick as a yard-brush all down his old back to the day of his death.' He dashed a manly tear away. 'Not but what I don't always feel quite up to the demands my lady friends make on me. Sometimes, Sir, it's like trying to shove a marshmallow into a money-box.'

'I know just what you mean,' I replied. We shook hands with emotion, he received a furtive tenner with dignity, Jock and I drove away. Everyone in the workshop was waving except the naughty apprentice who was wetting himself with recondite laughter. I think he used to think I *fancied* him, for God's sake.

Our progress to London Airport was almost royal; I found myself doing that wonderfully elliptical, downward-curving, quite inimitable wave that Her Majesty Queen Elizabeth the Queen Mother so excels at. One expected, naturally, a certain amount of *empressement* to be derived from hurrying noiselessly through London and its purlieus in £25,000 worth of pure white antique Rolls Royce, but I confess the merry laughter – the *holiday* mood – which our passage caused surprised me. It was not until we arrived at the Airport that I found the three inflated french letters, big as balloons, which the naughty apprentice had tied to our hood-stays.

At the Airport we found two surly, rat-faced men who denied that there ever was any such car, any such flight, any such *airline* even. Jock finally lumbered out of the driving seat and said two short and dirty words to them, whereupon the relevant documents were found in the twinkling of a bloodshot eye. I gave them a 'nicker' on Jock's advice and you'd have been surprised how smoothly the machinery rolled into motion. They drained the petrol out of the Rolls and disconnected the batteries. A beautiful young man with *huge* eyelashes emerged from some fastness and produced a pair of nippers from a leather case. He clipped little lead seals on to every openable aperture of the Ghost (which was already mounted on a pallet), then winked at Jock, sneered at me and flounced back to his embroidery.

A customs man who had been watching this came forward and took away all the bits of paper the F.O. man had given me. A dear little tractor hooked itself on to the pallet and chugged away with it. I've never seen a Rolls look so silly. That seemed to be that. Jock walked me to the Passenger Building and I let him buy me a drink, because he likes to keep his end up in public, then we bade each other gruff farewells.

My flight was announced by Donald Duck noises from a loudspeaker; I arose and shuffled off towards the statistical improbability of dying in an airplane crash. Personally, the thought of such a death appalls me little – what civilized man would not rather die like Icarus than be mangled to death on a Motorway by a Ford Popular?

When they let us undo our belts again a nice American sitting next to me offered me a huge and beautiful cigar. He was so diffident and called me 'Sir' so nicely that I had to take it. (It really was a lovely one, from the *atelier* of Henry Upmann.) He told me confidentially and impressively that meeting one's death in an airplane accident is a statistical improbability.

'Well, that's good news,' I tittered.

'Statistically,' he explained, 'you are in far greater hazard driving a three-year-old auto for eleven miles on a Freeway, according to the best actuaries.'

'Really,' I said – a word I only use when being told statistics by nice Americans.

'You can bet on it,' he said warmly. 'Personally, I fly many, many thousands of miles every year.'

'Well, there you are,' I said politely. 'Or rather, here you are, to prove the figures are right. What?'

'Exactly,' he said, drawing the word out.

We lapsed into a friendly silence, content with the rightness of our thinking, our cigars, teatlike, comforting our fears as our great gray dray horse of metal sped across St. George's Channel on its bright and battering sandals. After a while he leaned towards me.

'But just before take-off,' he murmured, 'don't your ass-hole pucker just a leetle?'

I thought about it carefully.

'More on landing, really,' I said at last, 'which is all wrong when you come to think about it.'

He thought about it for several minutes.

'You mean, like in an elevator?'

'Exactly.'

He guffawed happily, his own man again now, reassured that all men are sphincters at bottom, if I may coin a phrase.

Having settled the amenities, we got out our *work*, like two old women at a quilting-bee. Mine took the shape of a dreary German paperback on the Settecento in Naples (it takes a German *kunstkenner* to make that epoch dull) while he unzipped a document case full of computer paper, infinitely incomprehensible. I battled for a while with Professor Aschloch's tulgey prose – only German poets have ever written lucid German prose – then closed my eyes, wondering bitterly which of my enemies the nice American worked for.

He had made one mistake in an otherwise flawless performance: he hadn't told me his name. Have you ever exchanged three words with an American without being told his name?

I seemed to have made a great many enemies since Wednesday. The likeliest and nastiest possibility, the one which caused most *puckering*, was Colonel Blucher's lot, whoever they were. Martland was a horrible bastard in his own insular way but he could never shake off that blessed British sense of perspective. The grim, unbelievably rich US Government Agencies were another matter. Too serious, too dedicated; they believe it's all real.

Acid digestive juices, triggered by angst, started to slosh about in my stomach and uneasy gurgles came from the small intestine. I positively welcomed the stewardess with her tray of pallid garbage; I shovelled the stuff down like a starving man while my nice American waved his away, all jaded and travelled and statistically improbable.

Ulcer appeased for the nonce by plastic smoked salmon, rubber chop in vitreous aspic, chicken turd wrapped in polystyrene bacon and weeping half-thawed strawberry on dollop of shaving soap, I felt able to examine the possibility that I might be mistaken and that the man was, after all, just a wholesome American dolt. (Like a British dolt, really, only with better manners.)

Why, after all, should anyone want to plant such a man on me? What could I get *up* to on the journey? What, if it came to that, could *he* get up to on the journey? Extract a confession from me? Prevent me seizing command of the aircraft or overthrowing the Constitution of the United States? Surely, too, it would be a waste of an agent, for after several hours of propinquity I could scarcely fail to recognize him in the future. No; clearly, he must be what he seemed, an indifferent-honest executive, perhaps one of that super research firm which sells the State Department advice on where to start its next minor war. I turned to him, warm and relaxed, with new confidence. A man who smokes Upmanns cannot be all bad.

'I say, forgive me, but what are you doing?' I asked, in as British a way as I could muster. Gladly, he folded up the concertina of computer paper he had been grappling with (easy, though, for anyone who can handle an American Sunday newspaper) and turned amiably toward me.

'Why, I've been uh correlating and uh collating and uh evaluating this very, very complete printout of costs-sales data on a retail multiplex in uh Great Britain, Sir,' he explained candidly.

I continued to look at him, eyebrows hoisted a little, tiny, polite British question-marks shimmering from my hairline.

'Fish and chips,' he explained. I dropped the lower jaw a bit, achieving, I felt, an even more British effect.

'Fish and chips?'

'Right. I'm thinking of buying it.'

'Oh. Really. Er, much of it?'

'Well, yeah, kind of, all of it.' I made interested, interrogatory faces and he went on, and on. It appeared that fish and chips represent the last £100M industry in Britain still unclobbered and that he was about to clobber it. Seventeen thousand friers, almost all independent and many of them only marginally profitable, using 'half a million tons of fish, a million tons of potatoes and 100 thousand tons of fat and oil. They use, he told me, whatever fish their 'sender' chooses to sell them and pay whatever they have to; frying the stuff, for the most part, in oil which a Hottentot would spurn as a sexual lubricant. He painted a grisly picture of the present and a rosy one of the future, when he would have bought all the shops and franchised them back on his terms.

It all seemed to make very good sense and I decided, as he droned usefully on, that I would provisionally believe him to be genuine at least until we landed. In fact we rather chummed up, to the point where he asked me to come and stay at his apartment. Well, of course, I didn't believe in him that much, so I'm afraid I told him that I would be staying at the British Embassy. He looked at me thoughtfully, then told me about his dream of getting a duke to be chairman of his English company.

'Capital idea!' I said heartily, 'Can't have too many of them. Wonderful little workers, every one. Mind you, there's pretty stiff competition for your actual dukes today; even the merchant banks can't seem to hold them any more, they're all going into the menagerie trade as fast as they can. They may creep out into the open again now that Wilson's gone, of course, but if I were you I'd settle for a marquess or a brace of earls: far more of them about and they're much less uppity.'

'Earls?' he said. 'Say, do you by any chance know the Earl of Snowdon?' His eyes shone with innocence but I started like a guilty thing upon a fearful summons.

'Certainly not,' I twittered, 'no no no. He's something quite different again; anyway he's got a job, at the Design Centre I think, terrible lot there, except him of course, designs elephant aviaries for the Zoo, jolly good ones I'm sure. Very capable. Capital fellow. Happily married; dear little wife. Yes.' I subsided. He ground on implacably.

'Parm me, but are you an aristocrat?'

'No no no,' I said again, wriggling with embarrassment, 'nothing of the sort. Rotten shot. I'm only a nobleman and my brother bagged the only title: my father sort of dropped me a courtesy, ha ha.' He looked puzzled and distressed so I tried to explain.

'England isn't like the Continent, you see, nor even like Scotland in this respect. The *seize quartiers* "noble in all his branches" thing is something we don't like to talk about and there aren't half a dozen families with straight descent from a knight of the Conquest, I should think – and they aren't titled. Anyway,' I rambled on, 'no one in his senses would want to be descended from one of that lot: the Conquest was something between a joint-stock company and a Yukon gold-rush; William the Conk himself was a sort of primitive Cecil Roberts and his followers were bums, chancers, queers and comic singers.'

He was boggling beautifully now, so I couldn't resist going on.

'Broadly speaking, practically none of the aristocracy are peers today and very few of the peers are aristocrats by any standard which would be taken seriously on the Continent: most of them are lucky if they can trace their family back to some hard-faced oick who did well out of the Dissolution of the Monasteries.'

This really upset him; one end of his concertina of printouts escaped from his lap and cascaded on to the floor between our feet. We both stooped for it but I, being thinner than he by an inch or two, stooped lower, so that our heads did not actually ring together; but my nose (Norman, with Roman remains) found itself half inside his jacket and practically nuzzling the black butt of an automatic pistol in a shoulder clip.

'Ooops!' I squeaked, quite unnerved. He chuckled kindly, fatly.

'Don't you give that iron no never-mind, son; why, we Texans feel kind of undressed without one of them things.'

We chattered on in a desultory way but I found it hard to concentrate on the prettier points of fish-frying. Texas businessmen doubtless often carry pistols but I found it hard to believe that they would favour the inconvenient length of a Colt's Woodsman, which is a small calibre, long-barrelled automatic used only for target shooting and, more rarely, by professional killers who know they can plant its small bullet in just the right place. As a handy weapon of self-defence for the ordinary citizen it simply doesn't exist. Moreover, Texas businessmen, I felt sure, would be unlikely to house their pistols in Bryson rapid-release spring-clips.

The journey seemed to get longer all the time, if you follow me. The United States seemed distant and undesirable. As we landed the nice American finally told me his name – Brown, spelt b.r.a.u.n, pronounced Brawn. 'A likely story,' I thought. We farewelled and, a moment after we left the plane, he vanished. Once his warm and portly presence was gone I found I liked him less and less.

Martland had fulfilled my list of instructions faithfully – he would make someone a lovely wife. There was a big sad chap to meet me who guided me to an echoing bay where the Rolls stood and shimmered on its pallet, surrounded by other chaps with dear little petrol tankers, exotic licence plates, books of travellers' cheques and I don't know what-all. Oh yes, and a grave chap who struck my passport savagely with a rubber stamp. I accepted all their offerings with a weary courtesy, like a Crowned Head receiving specimens of native handicraft. There was also a furious little mannikin from the British Embassy but he was on the other side of a sort of pig-wire barrier – he had neglected to get the right sort of pass or something and the big, impassive Americans ignored his squeakings and gibberings completely, as did I. The chap with the petrol tanker wrenched the necessary lead seals off with pliers and tossed them through the wire to the squeaking chap as one throws peanuts to a zoo-bound ape, making vulgar clicking noises with his tongue and pretending to scratch his armpits. I began to fear for his health – the squeaking chap I mean, not the petrol chap.

I mounted the Rolls, sucking my lungs full of that unparalleled smell of new coachwork, new hide upholstery. The big sad chap, knowing his place, stood on the running-board to guide me out. The Rolls started up gently, gladly, like a well-goosed widow, and we drifted out of the Goods Area making about as much noise as a goldfish in a bowl. I could tell by the looks on their rough, untutored American faces that, had they been brought up in another culture, they would have been knuckling their foreheads. As a mark of respect, d'you see.

At the exit we were met by the chap from the Embassy, still squeaking and now well-nigh self-strangled with rage and chagrin. Had he been brought up in another culture he would probably have knuckled *my* forehead to some purpose. I reasoned with him, begging him to be a credit to the Corps Diplomatique, and he at last rallied. What it all boiled down to was that the Ambassador was at some Xanadu-like golf links far away, playing golf or rounders or something with one of their Presidents or Congressmen or whatever they are, but that he would be back in the morning, when I must report to him, shit or bust and cap in hand, to receive his admonitions and surrender my Greyhound and that he, the squeaker, demanded to know the name of the *bloody* man who had dared to tamper with the leaden Foreign Office seals on the Rolls. I told him that the chap's name was McMurdo (for the spur of the moment not bad, you must agree) and promised to try to find time to call on the Ambassador perhaps during the next few days.

He started getting incoherent again and kept beginning sentences with the words 'Do you realize . . .' and not finishing them, so I set my face against him.

'Pull yourself together,' I told him sternly, pressing a pound note into his hand. As I drove away I caught a glimpse of him in the driving mirror; he was jumping up and down on something. Too emotional by half, some of these diplomatic chaps. He'd be no good in Moscow, they'd have him compromised in a trice.

I found my hotel and handed over the Rolls to an able-looking brownish chap in the garage: he had a witty twinkle in his eye, I took to him instantly. We agreed that he could use only the duster on the coachwork and nothing else: Mr Spinoza would have haunted me if I'd let his Special Secret Wax be scoured with detergents or ossified with silicones. Then I rode the elevator – as they say over there, did you know? – up to the reception desk (my bags with me) and so by easy stages to a well-appointed suite with a lavatory worthy of the goddess Cloaca herself. Like a true-born Englishman I turned the ridiculous air conditioning off and threw open the windows.

Fifteen minutes later I turned the air conditioning back on and had to telephone the desk to send someone up to close the windows for me, oh the shame of it.

Later on they sent me up some sandwiches which I didn't much like.

Later still I read myself to sleep with one half-comprehended paragraph.

9

Does he stand stock-still henceforth? Or proceed
Dizzily, yet with course straightforward still,
Down-trampling vulgar hindrance? – as the reed
Is crushed beneath its tramp when that blind will
Hatched in some old-world beast's brain bids it speed
Where the sun wants brute-presence to fulfil
Life's purpose in a new far zone, ere ice
Enwomb the pasture-track its fortalice.

The Two Poets of Croisic

Do you know, they brought me a cup of tea in the morning – and jolly good tea it was too. If I could remember the name of the hotel I'd tell you.

Then they gave me one of those delicious elaborate American breakfasts, all sweet bacon and hotcakes and syrup and I didn't like it really.

I rode the elevator (!) down to the garage to inquire after the Rolls which had, it seemed, passed a comfortable night. The brownish chap hadn't been able to resist washing the windows but only with soap and water, he swore, so I pardoned him and gave him of my plenty. Ten minutes later I was in an enormous taxi-cab, an air-conditioned one, hired for the day for fifty dollars; it seems an awful lot, I know, but money's worth awfully little over there, you'd be surprised. It's because there's so much of it, you see.

The driver's name seemed to be Bud and somehow he'd got the notion that mine was Mac. I explained amicably that it was, in fact, Charlie, but he replied:

'Yeah? Well, that's very nice, Mac.'

I didn't mind after a while – I mean, when in *Rome*, eh? – and soon he was driving me round the sights of Washington, sparing nothing. It is a surprisingly splendid and graceful city, although built largely of a grotty kind of limestone; I loved every minute. The great heat was tempered by an agreeable little breeze which whipped the girls' cotton frocks about in the most pleasing way. How is it that American girls all contrive to have such appetizing legs; round, smooth, sturdily slender? If it comes to that, how is it that they all have such amazing tits? Bigger, perhaps, than you and I like them, but nonetheless delicious. When we stopped for a traffic light, a particularly well-nourished young person crossed in front of us, her stupendous mammaries jouncing up and down quite four inches at each step.

'My word, Bud,' I said to Bud, 'what an entrancing creature, to be sure!'

'Ya mean de dame wit de big knockers? Nah. In bed, they'd kinda spread out like a coupla fried eggs, king-size.'

The thought made me feel quite faint. He went on to give me a summary of his personal tastes in these matters, which I found fascinating but *bizarre* to a degree.

It has been suggested, with some truth, that Van Dyck's work when he was at Genoa constitutes the best group of portraits in the world. I came round to this point of view myself in the National Gallery at Washington: until you have seen their *Clelia Cattaneo* you can scarcely claim to have seen anything. I stayed an hour only in the Gallery: you can't absorb much art of that richness at one sitting, and I'd really only intended to look at one particular Giorgione. Had I but time as this fell sergeant Death is swift in his arrest, I could have unfolded a tale or two about it, but that shot is no longer on the board.

Emerging, already half drunk on injudiciously mixed art, I directed Bud to drive me to a typical lower-middle-class saloon for a cold beer and a bite of luncheon.

At the entrance Bud looked at me dubiously, up and down, and suggested that we try somewhere 'classier'.

'Nonsense, my dear Bud,' I cried staunchly, 'this is the normal, sober garb or kit of an English gentleman of fashion about to pay a call on his country's Envoy *in partibus* and I am sure it is well-known to these honest Washington folk. In Sir Toby's valiant words: "These clothes are good enough to drink in, and so be these boots, too." Lead on.'

He shrugged, in the expressive way these chaps have, and led duly on. He was very big and strong-looking but people nevertheless stared a little – he was dressed a bit informally perhaps, as cabbies often are, while I, as I have said, was correctly clothed as for interviewing ambassadors, merchant bankers and other grandees. In England no one would have remarked the contrast between us but they have no idea of democracy in America. Odd, that.

We ate in a sort of stall or booth, rather like the old-fashioned London chop house but flimsier. My steak was quite lovely but embarrassingly large: it seemed to be a cross-section through an ox. I had a salad with mine but Bud ordered a potato – *such* a potato; a prodigious tuber bred, he told me, on the plains of Idaho. I suppose I left about ten ounces of my steak and Bud quite coolly told the waiter (*his* name was Mac, too) to wrap it up for his dog and the waiter didn't even flicker although they both knew quite well that it would constitute Mrs Bud's supper that night. Steak is fearfully dear in Washington, as I daresay you know.

Bud may have licked me at the steak eating but I had him whipped at the liquor drinking. They have something there called, obscurely, High Balls, which we moved on to after our beer; he was no match for me at that game, quite outclassed. He eyed me, in fact, with a new respect. I believe I asked him to come and stay with me in London at one stage; at least I know I meant to.

As we left the bar a rather droll-looking citizen swayed across my path and asked, 'Whaddaya, some kinova nut or sumpn?' to which I replied in a matey phrase which I had heard Bud use to a fellow cabbie earlier in the day, as follows:

'Ah, go blow it out your ass!' (*A man hath joy by the answer of his mouth; and a word spoken in due season, how good it is!* Prov. XV: 23.)

To my dismay and puzzlement, the drunk chap took exception, for he hit me very hard in the face, making my nose bleed freely down my shirt. Vexed at this, I fear I retaliated.

When I was in one of those joke-and-dagger units in the war – yes, the *Second* World War, chicks – I went on one of those unarmed combat courses and, do you know, I was frightfully good at it, though you wouldn't think it to look at me.

I popped the heel of my hand under his nose – so much better than a punch – then toed him hard in the cobblers and, as he quite understandably doubled up, drove my knee into what was left of his poor face. He sort of fell down, not unnaturally in the circumstances, and as a precaution I stamped on each of his hands as I stepped over him. Well, he did hit me first, you know as I'm sure he'd be the first to admit. Bud, *enormously* impressed, hustled me outside while the saloon behind us applauded – pit, circle and gallery. An unpopular bloke, no doubt. I had very little trouble getting into the cab, although the driver's seat had changed sides again.

All the beautiful young men at the Embassy hated me on sight, nasty little cupcakes, but they passed me through to the Ambassador with no more delay than was necessary to make them feel important. The Ambassador received me in his shirt sleeves, if you'll believe it, and he, too, didn't seem to fancy me much. He accepted my courtly, old-world salutations with what I can only describe as a honk.

Now, for most practical purposes the ordinary consumer can divide Ambassadors up into two classes: the thin ones who tend to be suave, well-bred, affable; and the fleshier chaps who are none of these things. His present Excellency definitely fell into the latter grade: his ample mush was pleated with fat, wormed with the great pox and so besprent with whelks, bubukles and burst capillaries that it seemed like a contour map of the Trossachs. His great plum-coloured gobbler hung slack and he sprayed one when he spoke. I couldn't find it in my heart to love him but, poor chap, he was probably a Labour appointment: his corridors of power led only to the Gents.

'I won't beat about the bush, Mortdecai,' he honked, 'you are clearly an awful man. Here we are, trying to establish an image of a white-hot technological Britain, ready to compete on modern terms with any jet-age country in the world and here you are, walking about Washington in a sort of Bertie Wooster outfit as though you were something the Tourist Board had dreamed up to advertise Ye Olde Brytysshe Raylewayes.'

'I say,' I said, 'you pronounced that last bit marvelously.'

'Moreover,' he ground on, 'your ridiculous bowler is dented, your absurd umbrella bent, your shirt covered with blood and you have a black eye.'

'You should see the other feller?' I chirruped brightly, but it didn't go down a bit well. He was in his stride now.

'The fact that you are quite evidently as drunk as a fiddler's bitch in no way excuses a man of your age' – a nasty one, that – 'looking and behaving like a fugitive from a home for alcoholic music-hall artistes. I know little of why you are here and I wish to know nothing. I have been asked to assist you if possible, but I have not been instructed to do so: you may assume that I shall not. The only advice I offer is that you do not apply to this Embassy for help if and when you outrage the laws of the United States, for I shall unhesitatingly disown you and recommend imprisonment and deportation. If you turn right when you leave this room you will see the Chancery, where you will be given a receipt for your Silver Greyhound and a temporary civil passport in exchange for your Diplomatic one, which should never have been issued. Good day, Mr Mortdecai.'

With that, he started grimly signing letters or whatever it is that Ambassadors grimly sign when they want you to leave. I considered being horribly sick on his desk but feared that he might declare me a Distressed British Subject there and then, so I simply left the room in a marked manner and stayed not upon the order of my going. But I turned left as I went out of the room, which took me into a typists' pool, through which I strolled debonairly, twirling my brolly and whistling a few staves of 'Show Us Your Knickers, Elsie.'

I found Bud asleep in the parking lot and he drove me to a nearby saloon, in fact to more than one. I remember one particular place where a portly young woman took off her clothes to music, while dancing on the bar counter within reach of my hand. I had never seen an ecdysiast before; toward the end she was wearing nothing but seven beads, four of them sweat. I think that was the place we were chucked out of.

I know I went to bed but I must admit the details are a bit fuzzy: I'm not sure I even brushed my teeth.

10

Then we began to ride. My soul
Smoothed itself out, a long-cramped scroll
Freshening and fluttering in the wind.
Past hopes already lay behind.
The Last Ride Together

I awoke feeling positively chipper but the feeling didn't last. By the time I had dressed and packed I was being shaken with hangover like a rat in the grip of a keen but inexperienced terrier. I made it down to the hotel bar by easy stages (take the slow lift, never the express one) and the barman had me diagnosed and treated in no time at all. Your actual hangover, he explained, is no more than a withdrawal syndrome; halt the withdrawal by injecting more of what is withdrawing and the syndrome vanishes with a rustle of black wings. It seemed to make good sense. His prescription was simply Scotch and branch water – he swore a great oath that the branch water was freighted in fresh and fresh each morning from the Appalachian mountains, would you believe it? I tipped him with no niggardly hand.

Well medicated, but by no means potted, I paid my bill at the desk, collected a spotless Silver Ghost from a reluctant brownish chap and drove carefully away in the general direction of New Mexico. Posterity will want to know that I was wearing my Complete American Disguise: a cream tussore suit, sunglasses and a cocoa-coloured straw hat with a burnt-orange ribbon. The effect was pretty sexy, I don't mind telling you. Mr Abercrombie would have *bitten* Mr Fitch if he'd seen it and the *Tailor and Cutter* would have been moved to tears.

Curiously, I was afraid again. I felt obscurely that this land – 'where law and custom alike are based on the dreams of spinsters' – was nevertheless a land where I might well get hurt if I were not careful – or even if I were careful.

By the time that I was quite clear of the city's unlovely faubourgs and purlieus I needed petrol: the Silver Ghost is a lovely car but its best friend would have to admit that its m.'s per g. are few. I selected a petrol station that looked as though it could use the business and drew up. This was near a place called Charlottesville on the edge of the Shenandoah National Park. The attendant was standing with his back to me, arms akimbo, saying, 'Howd'ya like that guy?' and staring after a large powder-blue car which was vanishing at great speed down the road. He didn't realize my presence until I switched off the engine, then he double-took the Rolls in the most gratifying way, whispering 'shee-*it!*' again and again. (I was to hear enough admiring 'shee-its' in the next few days to refertilize the entire Oklahoma dust bowl.) He giggled like a virgin as he dipped the nozzle into the petrol tank and sped me on my way with one last dungy praise spattering my ears. I wondered vaguely what the powder-blue car had done to earn his disapproval.

I got a little lost after that, but an hour later I hit Interstate Highway 81 at Lexington and made excellent time down through Virginia. Once over the State line into Tennessee I called it quits for the day and booked in at a Genuine Log Kabins Motel. The yellow-haired, slack-mouthed, fat-arsed landlady wiggled her surplus flesh at me in the most revolting way: she looked about as hard to get as a haircut and at about the same price. Everything in my Kabin was screwed to the floor: the landlady told me that newlyweds often furnish their entire apartments with stuff they steal from motels, they spend the whole night unscrewing things, she told me with a coy giggle, indicating that she could think of better ways of passing the time. Like being screwed to the floor, I dare say.

The sheets were bright red. 'By golly,' I told them, 'I'd blush too, if I were you.'

For supper I had some Old Fashioned Mountain Boys' Corned Beef Hash; you'd think it would be delicious in Tennessee but it wasn't, you know; not a patch on Jock's. I drank some of my store of Red Hackle De Luxe and went to sleep instantly – you'd never have unscrewed *me*.

You can't get an early morning cup of tea in an American motel, not even for ready money; I wished I had brought a portable apparatus along. You've no idea how hard it is to get dressed without a cheering cup inside you. I hobbled to the restaurant and drank a whole pot of their coffee, which was excellent and nerved me to try the sweet Canadian bacon and hot cakes. Not at all bad, really. I noticed that the owner of the powder-blue car – or one very like it – had selected the same motel, but I didn't see him, or her. I idly wondered whether they'd done much unscrewing. For my part, I checked out with a clear conscience, I hadn't stolen anything for days.

I hardly got lost at all that morning. I was on US 40 in not much more than an hour and sailed clear across Tennessee on it, wonderful scenery. I had lunch in Nashville: spareribs and spoon bread and the finest jukebox I ever saw: it was a privilege to sit in front of it. Dazed with hot pork and decibels I nearly stepped under the wheels of a powder-blue car as I stepped off the sidewalk (pavement). Now, at the last count I'm sure there were probably half a million powder-blue cars in the United States, but when pedestrians walk under their wheels American drivers usually turn a bit powder-blue themselves and lean out and curse you roundly, calling you 'Buster' if you happen to be at all portly. This one did not: he looked through me and drove on, a thick-set, jowly chap rather like my Mr Braun, the crown prince of fish and chips, but hatted and sunglassed to the point of anonymity.

I dismissed the incident front my mind until I reached the outskirts of Memphis late that evening, when I was overtaken by just such a car driven by just such a chap.

They brought me coffee in my hotel room that night and a bottle of branch water for my Scotch; I locked the door and put in a call to Mr Krampf. American telephonists are wonderful, you just tell them the name and address of the chap you want to talk to and they do the rest. Krampf sounded a bit tight but very friendly; there was a lot of noise in the background which suggested that he had guests with him who were also a bit tight. I told him that I was on schedule, making no reference to his departure from our original plan.

'Well, that's just dandy,' he bellowed. 'Just dandy.' He said it a few times more, he's like that.

'Mr Krampf,' I went on guardedly, 'I seem to have a sort of companion on the road, if you know what I mean. A late model, powder-blue Buick convertible with New York plates. Do you have any idea . . .?

There was a long pause, then he chuckled fruitily.

'That's awright, son, that's your kind of escort. Wouldn't want anyone hijacking that old Rolls and Royce of mine.'

I made relieved noises and he went on: 'Hey, let's don't let him know we tumbled him, just make like he wasn't there and when he gets here and tells me you never made him I'll chew his nuts off, huh?'

'All right, Mr Krampf,' I said, 'but don't be too hard on him, will you. I mean, I was rather on the *qui vive*, you know.'

He delivered another fruity chuckle – or perhaps it was a belch – and rang off. Then somebody else rang off. Perhaps it was just the hotel telephonist, but the noises weren't quite right for that. Then I rang off and treated myself to a belch, too, and went to bed.

Nothing else happened that night, except that I worried a lot. Krampf hadn't made his millions by being a drunken old fart; to be a millionaire you need brains, ruthlessness and a certain little maggot in your brain. Krampf had all these and he was cleverer than me and much more evil. This was all wrong. My bowels whined and grumbled, they wanted to go home. Above all, they wanted no part in assassinating clever millionaires in their own homes. I finally nagged myself to sleep.

11

Yet now I wake in such decrepitude
As I had slidden down and fallen afar,
Past even the presence of my former self,
Grasping the while for stay at facts which snap,
Till I am found away from my own world,
Feeling for foot-hold through a blank profound,
Along with unborn people in strange lands . .

A Death in the Desert

It was Sunday but you'd never have thought so by what was going on when I got to Little Rock, Arkansas. Some sort of protest was going on and, as usual, short-haired chaps in dark blue were boredly biffing longhaired chaps in pale blue jeans, who were calling them pigs and throwing stones and things. All very sad. As a Russian said a hundred years ago, these people believe that they are the doctors of society, whereas in fact they are only the disease. Traffic was at a standstill and, several cars ahead of me, I could see the blue Buick, bogged down in a sea of long hair and flourishing riot sticks.

I killed the engine and mused. Why the devil would Krampf go to the expense and trouble of escorting across half a continent a motor car which no one in his senses would attempt to steal – and escorting it in so curiously oblique a way? Setting aside the strong possibility that he was barmy, I decided that he must have told someone about the extra piece of canvas which ought to be secreted about the car – *that* made him pretty barmy of course – and was now regretting it. Worse, he might be playing some deeper and more convoluted game, which would be consistent with his unscripted letter to the almost royal Chum. He could scarcely have guessed at the little murder job which Martland had entrusted to me but he might well have come to consider me, for other reasons, as sort of redundant and a threat to his security. 'The heart is deceitful about all things, and desperately corrupt; who can understand it?' cries Jeremiah XVII:9 and as you know, Jeremiah XVII:9 was a chap with great insight into these matters, as well as being a little barmy himself.

My little private store of worries and ass puckerings was much augmented by all this; I found myself pining for Jock's strong right arm and brass-garnished bunch of fives. The plot was thickening in a marked manner; if I could not soon lay hold of a spoon with which to stir it, there was a distinct danger that it might stick to the bottom. *My* bottom, probably. And then where would the Hon. C. Mortdecai be? There was a dusty answer to that one.

The traffic moved on after everyone concerned had been thoroughly biffed and bashed and screamed at and I didn't spot the Buick again until just after the Shawnee crossing of the North Canadian River, where I glimpsed it lurking down a side road. I stopped at the next petrol station (they call it gas there, I wonder why?) hoping to give the driver a good eyeballing as he passed.

What I saw made me gape and gibber like a housewife choosing Daz on the television; two or three seconds later I was twenty miles down the road, sitting on a motel bed and sucking in whisky until I could think straight. It was the same car – at least it bore the same number plates – but overnight it had lost a deep dent in a fender and acquired a suit of whitewall tires and another radio antenna. The driver had lost a few stones and become a thin, dyspeptic cove with a mouth like the slot in a piggy-bank. In short, it was not the same car at all. The implications were unclear but one thing stood out like Priapus: there was no way in which this could be a change for the better. Someone was devoting a good deal of time and trouble and expense to the affairs of C. Mortdecai and it certainly wasn't the Distressed Gentlefolk's Aid Society. A stupid man might not have been too frightened but I was not stupid enough for that. A really bright chap, on the other hand, would have dumped everything and run for home with all speed, but I was not really bright, either.

What I did was leave the motel, telling them that I would be back after dinner (I'd already paid, naturally) and drive circuitously to the heart of Oklahoma City, arriving tired and grim.

Not too near the centre I found a solid, sober sort of hotel which looked as though it would not knowingly harbour the more obvious kind of *barbouze* or assassin. I drove into the underground garage and waited until the night attendant had exhausted his stock of admiring 'shee-its', then I told him that the Rolls was entered in an RR *Concours d'Elégance* in Los Angeles the following week and that a hated rival would stop at nothing to impede my progress or the car's chances of success.

'What would you do,' I asked him hypothetically 'if a stranger offered you money to let him sit in the car for five minutes while you went away and sat in your office?'

'Well, Sir,' he said, 'I guess I'd jest wave this little old wrench at him and tell him to haul his ass out of here, then I'd ring the desk upstairs and then in the morning I'd kind of tell you how much money he'd offered me, see what I mean, Sir.'

'I do indeed. You are clearly a capital fellow. Even if nothing happens I shall assume, in the morning, that you refused let us say five, ah, *bucks*, what?'

'Thank you, Sir.'

I went up in the lift or elevator and started work on the desk clerk. He was a well-scrubbed, snotty little chap in one of those suits only desk clerks can buy – or would want – and his breath smelled of something unwholesome and probably illegal. He studied my luggage like a pawnbroker before he peevishly admitted that he did have a vacant room with bath, but he thawed fast when he saw my diplomatic passport and the five-dollar bill I had carelessly left inside it. He was just sliding the money towards him when I trapped it with a well-shaped forefinger. I leaned over the counter and lowered my voice.

'No one but you and I knows that I am here tonight. Do you follow me?'

He nodded, both our fingers still on the money.

'Consequently, anyone telephoning me will be trying to *locate* me. Are you still following?'

He still was.

'Now, none of my *friends* could possibly be trying to get in touch with me here and my enemies are members of a political party which is dedicated to the overthrow of the United States. So what will you do if somebody calls me?'

'Call the cops?'

I winced with unfeigned chagrin.

'No no NO,' I said. 'By no means the cops. Why do you think I'm *in* Oklahoma City?'

That really fetched him. Awe stole into his juicy eyes and his lips parted with a tiny plop.

'You mean, just call you? Sir?' he said at last.

'Right,' I said, and released the five dollars. He stared at me until I was inside the lift. I felt reasonably secure – desk clerks all over the world have two talents: selling information and knowing when not to sell information. These simple skills spell survival to them.

My room was large, well-proportioned and pleasant but the air conditioning made tiresome noises at random intervals. I asked room service for a selection of their best sandwiches, a bottle of branch water, a good drinking glass and the house detective. They all arrived together. I took pains to befriend the detective, who was an awkward, seven-foot youth with a shoulder holster which creaked noisily when he sat down. I gave him Scotch whisky and a load of old moody similar to that which the desk clerk had gobbled. He was a serious boy and asked for my credentials; they impressed him considerably and he promised to keep a special eye on my floor that night.

When he had gone, five dollars later, I inspected my sandwiches with moody pleasure; there was great store of them, on two sorts of bread and filled with all manner of good things: I did my best with them, drank some more Scotch and got into bed, feeling that I had secured myself as best I could.

I shut my eyes and the air conditioner rushed into my head, carrying with it all manner of dread and speculation, a thousand horrid fancies and a mounting panic. I dared not take a sleeping pill. After an interminable half hour I gave up the fight for sleep and put the light on. There was only one thing for it – I lifted the telephone and put in a call to Mrs Spon in London. London, England, that is.

She came through in a mere twenty minutes, shrieking and honking with rage at being awakened and swearing by strange gods. I could hear her vile little poodle Pisse-Partout in the background, adding his soprano yelps to the din; it made me quite homesick.

I soothed her with a few well chosen words and she soon got it into her head that this was a matter of some seriousness. I told her that, at all costs, Jock must be at the *Rancho de los Siete Dolores* by Tuesday and that she must see to it. She promised. The problem of getting an American visa in a few hours is nothing to a woman like her: she once got a private audience of the Pope just by knocking on the door and saying she was expected; they say he very nearly gave her a contract to redo the Sistine Chapel.

Knowing that Jock would be there to meet me eased my worst fears, it only remained now to get there without leaving any bloodstains in my spoor.

I sank into an uneasy slumber interspersed, curiously, with erotic dreams.

12

There was no tea to be had in the morning but I was on the very threshold of the old West and knew that I had to learn to rough it. 'Pioneers! Oh, Pioneers!' as Walt Whitman never tired of exclaiming.

Neither the desk nor the garage had anything to report, so I toddled out to take the air and see if the neighbourhood was blue-Buick-infested. What I found was a sort of bar advertising in its window something called the Old Oklahoma Cattleman's Breakfast Special. Who could resist it? Not I.

The O.O.C.B.S. proved to be a thick steak, almost raw, a hunk of salt bacon the size and shape of my fist, a pile of hot sourdough biscuits, a tin pot of ferocious coffee and half a gill of rye whisky. Now I am a man of iron, as you will by now have realized, but I confess I belched. I was trapped, for the barman and the short-order cook were both leaning on the bar, watching my future career with considerable interest as it were, their faces grave and courteous but sort of expectant. Britain's honour lay in pawn to my knife and fork. I weakened some of the coffee with some of the whisky and drank it, suppressing a gagging shudder. I found strength after this to try a hot biscuit, then some more coffee, then a corner of the bacon and so on. Appetite grew on what it fed upon and soon, to the amazement of myself and all beholders, the very steak itself fell to my bow and spear. 'Tis from scenes like this that Britain's greatness springs. I accepted a free drink from the barman, shook hands gravely and made a good exit. Not all Ambassadors sit in Embassies, you know.

Much fortified, I collected the Rolls and turned my face toward the Golden West, the Lyonesse of our times, the nursery of the great American fairy tale. At noon I crossed the State line into the panhandle of Texas, a solemn moment for any man who rode with the Lone Ranger each Saturday morning as a child.

Mindful of the Buick-mounted rustler on my trail, I started to buy a few gallons of petrol at almost every petrol station, taking care to inquire at each one for the road to Amarillo – which lay due West on that very road. Sure enough, the blue car swept by me somewhere between the townships of McLean and Groom, the driver looking neither to right nor left. Clearly, he was satisfied of my destination and intended to front-tail me to Amarillo. I let him have a few reassuring glimpses of me in his driving mirror, lying a mile behind him, then chose a useful left hand turning and sped south to Claude then southeast through Clarendon to the Prairie Dog Town fork of the Red River – there's a place name to stir the blood – which I crossed at Estelline. I felt no need of luncheon but kept up my strength with a little rye whisky here and there and an occasional egg to give it something to bite on. Following the least probable roads I worked my way West again and by mid-afternoon I was satisfied that I must have lost the Buick for good. Needless to say I had lost myself too, but that was of secondary importance. I found a sleepy motel staffed by one thirteen-year-old boy who hired me a cabin without raising his eyes from his comic book.

'Hail Columbia! Happy land!' I told him, borrowing freely from R.H. Horne, 'Hail, ye heroes! Heaven-born band!'

He almost looked up, but decided in favour of The Teenage Werewolf From Ten Thousand Fathoms – I couldn't find it in my heart to blame him.

I zizzed away the worst of the afternoon, awakening some three hours later with a mighty thirst. When I had seen to that I strolled outside to stretch my legs and scare up some ham and eggs. A furlong down the dusty road, under the shade of a valley cottonwood, stood a powder-blue Buick.

That settled it: the Rolls was bugged. No human agency could have tracked me through that mazey day unaided. Quite calm, I ate the bacon and shirred eggs along with great manly cups of coffee, then sauntered back to the Rolls with the air of a man quite unencumbered with powder-blue Buicks. It took me almost ten minutes to find the tiny transistorized tracer beacon: it was magnetized fiercely to the underside of my right hand front mudguard.

I started the Ghost and drifted away in the wrong direction; after a few miles I hailed, frantically, a State Trooper mounted on an unbelievable motor bike and proclaimed myself lost.

When a native son is unwise enough to ask the way of an American policeman he is either jailed for vagrancy or, if the policeman is a kindly one, told to buy a map. This one, I swear, would have *struck* me for flagging him down had I not been wearing an English accent and a Rolls Royce of great beauty, but these beguiled him into a *pro hac vice* civility. I got out of the car and, as he pointed things out to me on the map, leaned lightly against his great Harley Davidson machine, letting the grumble of the idling engine drown the smart click of the mini-transmitter's magnet as it clamped itself under his rear mudguard. He roared away northwards at a dashing pace; I lurked down a dirt road until the Buick dawdled by in confident pursuit, then off I went like the clappers, south and west.

A vast, theatrical moon rose over Texas and I drove on spellbound for hours through forests of Spanish Bayonet and fields of amaranthine sagebrush. At last, on the edge of the Llano Estacado, the Staked Plains themselves, I edged the Rolls into a friendly canyon and settled down to sleep behind the wheel, a bottle of whisky within easy reach in case of mountain lions.

Prompt on cue, a coyote curdled the thin distances of the night air with his whooping love song and, as I drifted into sleep, I thought I heard the muted thunder of far away, unshod hooves.

13

I met him thus:
I crossed a ridge of short broken hills
Like an old lion's cheek-teeth . . .
An Epistle

I was awakened by a shot.

Not thrilled? Then I venture to guess that you have never been awakened in that way yourself. For my part I found myself down among the accelerator and brake pedals before I was properly awake, whimpering with terror and groping frantically for the Banker's Special pistol in its hidey-hole under the seat.

Nothing happened.

I thumbed back the hammer and peeped, wincing, over the edge of the window.

Nothing went on happening.

I looked through the other windows – nothing – and decided that I had dreamed the shot, for my sleep had been illustrated with the dread exploits of Comancheros, Apaches, Quantrill's guerrillas and other fiends in human shape. I treated myself to another O.O.C.B.S. breakfast, only this time without the steak, ham, hot biscuits or coffee. There were one or two bad moments but I was not sick and the old rapture was soon recaptured and I felt emboldened to step out for *un petit promenade hygiénique*. As I opened the car door another shot rang out, followed one fifth of a second later by the bang of the car door closing again. There is still nothing wrong with the Mortdecai reaction time.

I listened carefully to my audile memory, recalling the exact noise of the shot.

1. It had not been the unmistakable, explicit BANG of a shotgun
2. Not the vicious CRACK of a small calibre rifle
3. Not the BOOM of a .45 pistol
4. Not the ear-stinging WHAM of a heavy calibre standard rifle, or a magnum pistol fired in your direction
5. Not the terrifying whip-crack WHANG-UP of a high velocity sporting rifle fired towards you, but something of the same nature
6. A sporting rifle, then, but
7. Not fired in the canyon because no echoes and surely
8. *Not fired at me* – dammit, a Girl *Guide* couldn't miss a Rolls Royce with two slowly aimed shots.

My intellect was satisfied that it was some honest rancher smartening up the local coyotes: my body took longer to pacify. I crept back on to the seat and twitched gently for fifteen minutes, nibbling at the rye from time to time. After about a hundred years I heard an old car start up miles away across the desert and chug even further away. I sneered at my craven self.

'You craven wretch,' I sneered. Inexplicably, I then fell asleep for another hour. Nature knows, you know.

It was still only nine o'clock when I set off on the last leg of my journey, feeling old and dirty and incapable. You probably know the feeling if you are over eighteen.

It is hard to drive in a cringing position but nevertheless I got the Rolls into its stride and strode across the Staked Plains at a good mile-munching pace. The Staked Plains are not really very exciting, when you've seen one Staked Plain you've seen them all. I particularly don't want to tell you where Krampf's rancho is – perhaps *was* now – but I don't mind admitting that it lay two hundred straightish miles from my overnight bivouac and between the Sacramento Mountains and the Rio Hondo. Just names on a map that morning, the poetry all gone. There's nothing like gunfire to drive the glamour from words. I soon became tired of the creosote bushes, desert willows and screw-beams, not to mention the eternal, giant cacti, so different from the ones Mrs Spon grows in her conservatoilette.

I entered New Mexico at noon, still unmolested, still feeling old and dirty. At Lovington (named after old Oliver Loving who blazed the fearful Goodnight-Loving trail in '66 and died along it of arrow wounds the following year) I had a bath, a shave, a change of raiment and a dish of *Huevos 'Ojos de Comanchero,'* which sounded lovely. In reality it was the most terrifying sight I had seen to date: two fried eggs decorated with ketchup, Tabasco and chopped chillis in the semblance of a pair of bloodshot eyes – I would as soon have eaten my own leg. I waved the grimly thing away; Old Oklahoma Cattlemen are one thing, but these were merely tetrous. I tried, instead, 'Chilli 'n' Franks' which proved to be rather good, just like chilli con carne but with dear little salty bangers instead of the ground meat. While I ate, various admiring *peons* were handwashing the Rolls, with soap 'n' water only, of course.

With a bare hundred miles to go, clean, dapper and now only middle-aged again, I pointed the Rolls' nose toward the Ranch of the Seven Sorrows of the Virgin, where I would lay down my pilgrim's scrip of care, my cockle-hat of fear and my staff of illegality; where, moreover, I would take delivery of a great deal of money and perhaps kill a Krampf. Or perhaps not. I had left England prepared to keep my part of the bargain with Martland, but I had thought a great deal during those hundreds of remorseless American miles and had evolved certain arguments against keeping faith with him. (We had never been *friends* at school after all, for he was the house tart, and known to one and all as 'Shagnasty': not for nothing does a boy acquire such a name.)

I had also bought a denser pair of sunglasses; my old ones were calculated for the lemonade-like rays of the English sun and were no proof against the brutal onslaught of the desert light. Even the shadows, razor edged, purple and green, were painful to look at. I drove with all windows shut and the side blinds drawn across: the inside of the Rolls was like an ill-regulated sauna bath but this was better than letting in the dry, scorching fury of the air outside. I was soon sitting in a distressful swamp of sweat and my old wound started to trouble me; chilli 'n' trepidation were playing the devil with my small intestines and my borborigmus was often louder than the engine of the Rolls, which loped on undeterred, quietly guzzling its pint of petrol per statute mile.

By mid-afternoon I was alarmed to notice that I had stopped sweating and had started talking to myself – and was listening. It was becoming difficult to distinguish the road amongst the writhing pools of heat-haze and I could not tell whether the scraggy-feathered road-runners were under my wheels or a furlong ahead of me.

Half an hour later I was on a dirt road under a spur of the Sacramento range, lost. I stopped to consult the map and found myself listening to the enormous silence – 'that silence where the birds are dead yet something singeth like a bird'.

From somewhere above me a shot was fired, but there was no sound of a bullet passing and I had no intention of cringing twice in one day. Moreover, there was no mistaking the nature of the firearm, it was the wholesome bark, flattened by the heavy air, of a large calibre pistol loaded with black powder. High on the ridge above me was a horseman waving a broad brimmed hat and already starting to descend with casual mastery of – and disregard for – his mount. *Her* mount, as it turned out, and what a mount. *¡Que caballo!* I knew what it was imme-diately, although I had never before seen the true *bayo naranjado* – the vivid orange dun with a pure white mane and tail. It was entire – no one, surely, could geld a horse like that – and came down the ragged rock slope as though it were Newmarket Heath. The low-horned, double-girthed Texas saddle was enriched with silver *conchos* over intricately tooled and inlaid leathers and the girl herself was dressed like a museum exhibit of Old Texas: low-crowned black Stetson with rattler band and woven-hair storm-strap, bandana with the ends falling almost to the waist, brown Levi's tucked into unbelievable Justin boots which were themselves tucked into antique silver Spanish stirrups and garnished with Kelly spurs fashioned, apparently, of gold.

She arrived at the foot of the slope in a small avalanche, reins slack, welded to her saddle with fierce thighs, and the stallion took the storm ditch as though it was not there, landing dramatically beside the Rolls in a spatter of stones.

I wound a window down and peered out with a polite expression. I was met with a spray of cheesy foam from the horse's mouth; it showed me some of its huge yellow teeth and offered to bite my face off, so I wound the window up again. The girl was inspecting the

Rolls; as her horse moved forward past the window I found myself staring at a beautiful gunbelt of Mexican work with *buscadero* holsters, containing a pair of pristine Dragoon-pattern Colts, the paper-cartridge model of the 1840s, with grips by Louis Comfort Tiffany – unmistakable – dating from perhaps twenty years later. She wore them correctly for the Southwest – butts forward, as though for the flashy Border cross-draw or the cavalry twist (much more sensible), and they were not tied down, of course – this was no Hollywood mock-up but a perfect historical reconstruction. (Try mounting or even trotting with pistols in open holsters tied down to your thighs.) From the saddle scabbard protruded, as was only fitting, the butt of a One-in-One-Thousand Winchester repeater.

From hat to horseshoes she must have been worth a fortune as she sat – it gave me a new vision of the uses of wealth – and that was not counting her splendid person, which looked even more valuable. I am not, as you may have guessed, especially keen on commonplace sex, especially with women, but this vision unequivocally stirred my soggy flesh. The silk shirt was pasted to her perfect form with delicate sweat, the Levi's made no bones about her pelvic delights. She had the perfect round hard bottom of the horsewoman but not the beamy breadth of the girl who started to ride too young.

I emerged from the other side of the car and addressed her across the bonnet – I am just enough of a horseman never to try to make friends with tired stallions on hot days.

'Good afternoon,' I said, by way of a talking point.

She looked me up and down. I sucked in my tummy. My face was as blank as I could make it but she knew, she knew. They know, you know.

'Hi,' she said. It left me gasping for air.

'Can you by any chance direct me to the *Rancho de los Siete Dolores?*' I asked.

Her bee-stung lips parted, the little white teeth opened a fraction; perhaps it was a sort of smile.

'What is the old auto worth?' she asked.

'I'm afraid it's not for sale, really.'

'You are stupid. Also overweight. But cute.' There was a hint of a foreign accent in her voice, but it was not Mexican. Vienna perhaps, perhaps Buda. I asked the way again. She raised the handle of her beautiful quirt to her eyes and scanned the Western horizon. It was one of those quirts with a bit of pierced horn let into the handle: more useful than a telescope in that climate. I began, for the first time, to understand Sacher-Masoch.

'Go that way right across lots,' she pointed, 'the desert is no worse than the road. Follow the bones when you come to them.'

I tried to think of another talking point but something told me she was not much of a chatterbox – indeed, even as I searched for a way to detain her she had flicked the thong of her quirt under the stallion's belly and was away into the shimmering jumble of baking rock. Well, you can't win them all. 'Lucky old saddle,' I thought.

In twenty minutes I came upon the first of the bones she had spoken of: the bleached skeleton of a Texas Longhorn artistically disposed beside a faint track. Then another and another, until I reached a huge ranch gateway in the middle of nowhere. Its sunbleached crossbar supported a great polychromed Mexican carving of an agonized Madonna and a board hung below into which had been burned the rancho's brand – two Spanish bits. I wondered whether there was a joke implied and decided that, if there was, it was not of Mr Krampf's making.

Past the gate the trail was well-defined; the buffalo grass became richer with every furlong and I began to get glimpses of groups of horseflesh crowded under the cottonwoods – Morgans, Palominos, Appaloosas and I don't know what-all. Occasional riders began to fall in casually behind and beside me: by the time I reached the huge, rambling *hacienda* itself I was escorted by quite a dozen *charro*-clad desperadoes, all pretending that I wasn't there.

The house was astonishingly beautiful, all white columns and porticoes, the outside a maze of green lawns, fountains, patios, flowering agaves and yuccas. The door of a carport rolled itself up unbidden and I gentled the Rolls in, between a Bugatti and a Cord. When I emerged, bags in hand, my escort of bandits had vanished upon some unheard summons and only a small, impertinent boy was visible. He fluted something in Spanish, whisked my luggage away from me and indicated a shady patio, to which I made my way in as elegant a fashion as my tortured trousers would allow.

I sat down on a marble bench, stretched luxuriously and rested my grateful eyes on the statuary half-hidden in the green shade. One statue, more weather-worn than the others, proved to be an ancient and immobile old lady, hands folded in lap, gazing at me incuriously. I leaped to my feet and bowed – she was the kind of woman to whom people would always accord bows. She inclined her head a little. I fidgeted. Clearly, this must be Krampf's mother.

'Have I the honour of addressing Mrs Krampf?' I asked at length.

'No, Sir,' she replied in the careful English of the well-taught foreigner, 'you address the Countess Grettheim.'

'Forgive me,' I said, sincerely, for which of us, not being a Krampf, would care to be mistaken for one?

'Are Mr and Mrs Krampf at home?' I asked.

'I could not say,' she replied serenely. The subject was evidently closed. The silence stretched out beyond the point where I dared do anything about it. If the old lady's mission in life was to prevent me feeling cosy, she was certainly in fine midseason form – '*si extraordinairement distinguée*' as Mallarmé used to say, '*quand je lui dis bonjour, je me fais toujours l'effet de lui dire "merde"*'.

I looked at the statues again. There was an excellent copy of the Venus Callipygea, on whose cool marble buttocks my eyes lingered gratefully. Determined not to be flustered, I succeeded so well that my sun-sore eyelids began to droop.

'Are you not thirsty?' the old lady suddenly asked.

'Eh? Oh, well, er – '

'Then why do you not ring for a servant?'

She knew bloody well why I did not ring for a servant, the old bitch. I did ring for one then, though, and a strapping hussy appeared wearing one of those blouses – you know, the ones with a sort of drawstring or rip-cord – bearing a tall glass full of something delicious.

I inclined politely toward the Countess before taking the first sip. This, too, proved a mistake, for she gave me a basilisk stare as though I'd said, 'Cheers, dears.'

It occurred to me that I should tell her my name, so I did and a certain limited thaw set in; clearly, I should have done this before.

'I am Mr Krampf's mother-in-law,' she said suddenly and her toneless voice and impassive face somehow carried words of contempt for people named Krampf. And for people named Mortdecai, too, for that matter.

'Indeed,' I said, with just a hint of polite incredulity in my voice.

Nothing happened for some time except that I finished my drink and summoned the courage to ring for another. She already had me summed up as a low-life; I felt she might as well know me for a toper as well.

Later, a barefoot peon crept in and mumbled to her in thick Spanish, then crept out again. After a while she said, 'My daughter is now in and wishes to see you,' then closed her parchment eyelids with finality. I was dismissed. As I left the patio I distinctly heard her say, 'You will have time to couple with her once before dinner, if you are quick.' I stopped as though I had been shot in the back. C. Mortdecai is not often at a loss for words but a loss is what he was at then. Without opening her eyes she went on – 'Her husband will not mind, he does not care to do it himself.'

There was still nothing in this for me. I let the words hang reverberating in the still air while I slunk away. A servant fielded me neatly as I entered the house and led me to a small tapestry-hung chamber on the first floor. I sank into the most sumptuous sofa you can imagine and tried to decide whether I was sunstruck or whether the old lady was the family loony.

You will not be surprised, percipient reader, to learn that when the tapestries parted the girl who entered the room was the girl I had seen on the stallion. I, however, was very surprised, for when I had last met Mrs Krampf – in London, two years before – she had been a villainous old boot wearing a ginger wig and weighing in at some sixteen stones. No one had told me that there was a later model.

Retrieving my eyes, which had been sticking out like chapel hat pegs, I started to scramble to my feet, making rather a nonsense of it what with my short legs and the unreasonably deep sofa. Upright at last, and rather cross, I saw that she was wearing what I suppose I shall have to describe as a Mocking Smile. Almost, one could imagine a red, red rose between her Pearly Teeth.

'If you call me "amigo,"' I snapped, 'I shall scream.' She raised an eyebrow shaped like a seagull's wing and the smile left her face.

'But I had no intention of being so, ah, *fresh*, Mr Mortdecai, nor do I care to ape the speech of these Mexican savages. The *pistolero valiente* disguise is a whim of my kooky husband' – she had a wonderfully fastidious way of using Americanisms – 'and the pistols are something to do with castration complexes: I do not care to understand, I have no interest in Dr Freud and his dirty mind.'

I had her placed now: Viennese Jewess, the loveliest women in the world and the cleverest. I pulled myself together.

'Forgive me,' I said. 'Please let us start again. My name is Mortdecai.' I put my heels together and bowed over her hand; she had the long and lovely fingers of her race and they were as hard as nails.

'Mine is Johanna. You know my married name.' I got the impression that she pronounced it as infrequently as possible. She motioned me back into the sofa – all her gestures were beautiful – and stood there, legs astride. Looking up at her from the depths of that bloody sofa was awkward; lowering my gaze I found myself staring at her jean-gripped crotch, fourteen inches from my nose. (I use fourteen in the Borgesian sense of course.)

'Those are beautiful pistols,' I said, desperately. She did something astonishingly swift and complicated with her right hand and, simultaneously it seemed, a Tiffany butt was six inches from my face. I took it from her respectfully – look, the Dragoon Colt is over a foot long and weighs more than four pounds: unless you've handled one you can't begin to understand the strength and skill you need to flip it about casually. This was an intimidating young woman.

It was indeed a very beautiful pistol. I spun the cylinder – it was loaded in all chambers but, correctly, one nipple was uncapped for the hammer to ride on. There was much splendid engraving and I was startled to see the initials J.S.M.

'Surely these did not belong to John Singleton Mosby?' I asked, awestruck.

'I think that was his name. A cavalry raider or something of that sort. My husband never tires of telling how much he paid for them – for myself, I forget, but it seemed an excessive amount.'

'Yes,' I said, cupidity stabbing me like a knife. 'But are these not rather big weapons for a lady? I mean, you handle them beautifully but I should have thought something like a Colt Lightning or the Wells Fargo model perhaps . . .

She took the pistol, checked the position of the hammer and prestidigitated it back into the holster.

'My husband insists on these big ones,' she said, boredly. 'It is something to do with the castration complex or the organ inferiority or some such nastiness. But you must be thirsty, my husband tells me you are *often* thirsty, I shall bring you some drink.' With that she left me. I began to feel a bit castrated myself.

She was back in about two minutes, having changed into a minimal cotton frock and followed by a drinks-laden peon. Her manner, too, had changed and she sank down beside me with a friendly smile. *Close* beside me. I sort of inched away a bit. Cringed away would be better. She looked at me curiously for a moment, then giggled.

'I see. My mother has been talking to you. Ever since she caught me when I was seventeen wearing nothing under my dress she has been convinced that I am a mare in heat. It is not true.' She was making me a large, strong drink – the peon had been dismissed. 'On the other hand,' she continued, handing me the glass with a dazzling smile, 'I have an unaccountable passion for men of your age and build.' I simpered a little, making it clear that I recognized a joke and perhaps a mild *tease*.

'Tee hee,' I said. Then 'Aren't you having a drink?'

'I never drink alcohol. I do not like to blunt my senses.'

'Goodness,' I babbled, 'but how awful for you. Not drinking, I mean. I mean, imagine getting up in the morning knowing that you're not going to feel any better all day.'

'But I feel lovely all day, every day. Feel me.' I spilled quite a lot of my drink.

'No, really,' she said, '*feel*.'

I gingerly prodded a golden, rounded forearm.

'Not there, stupid: here!' She flipped a button open and two of the most beautiful breasts in the world sprang out, quite bare, hard and richly nippled. In all civility I could not decline to grasp one, indeed, my hand made the decision for me. My castration complex had vanished like an evil dream. She pulled my head down to her.

Much as I enjoy kissing girls' nipples, I must say I usually feel a bit sheepish about it, don't you? I'm reminded of fat old men sucking juicily at their teat-like cigars. However, the extravagance of Johanna's response to my first tentative grazing on her lovely pastures was such as to dispel all embarrassment from my mind, replacing it with fears for my own health. She reared up like a tortured cat and wrapped herself around me as though she were in the last extremities of drowning. Her slim, calloused fingers grasped me with delicious ferocity and I soon ascertained that her policy on underwear had not changed since she was seventeen.

'Wait,' I said urgently, 'shouldn't I take a shower first? I'm filthy.'

'I know,' she snarled, 'I love it. You smell like a horse. You *are* a horse.'

Obediently, I broke into a canter, urged by her drumming heels. I was glad she had taken her spurs off.

Descriptions of middle-aged art dealers being ravished are neither instructive nor edifying, so I shall draw a row of *'frissons'* like a shower curtain across the extraordinary scene which followed. Here they are:

. . . .

I was shown to my room by the barefooted hussy in the drawstring blouse. She smiled at me blandly, pointing her lavish bosom like a pair of pistols.

'I am at your service while you stay at the Rancho, señor,' she said guilelessly. 'My name is Josefina – that is, like Josephine.'

'How apt,' I murmured, 'in the circumstances.'

She didn't get it.

As the Countess had predicted, I was just in time for dinner. Changed and bathed, I sat down feeling more like the C. Mortdecai we know and love but I admit to having felt a little chary, a little *coy* about meeting the old lady's eye. As it happened, she avoided catching mine; she was a dedicated food eater, it was a pleasure to sit in front of her.

'Tell me,' I said to Johanna as the second course appeared, 'where is your husband?'

'He is in his bedroom. Next to the little dressing room where I, ah, received you.'

I stared at her in panic – no sensate human being could have slept through the zoo-like racket of our coupling. Seeing my consternation she laughed merrily.

'Please do not worry about it. He did not hear a thing, he has been dead several hours.'

I don't really remember what we had for dinner. I'm sure it was delicious but I seemed to have difficulty swallowing and I kept on dropping knives, forks and things. 'Quaking' is the only word for what I was doing. All I remember is the old Countess opposite me, cramming the groceries into her frail body like one who provisions a yacht for a long voyage. '*Cur quis non prandeat hoc est*?' seemed to be her attitude.

We had reached the port and walnuts stage before I recovered enough aplomb to venture another question.

'Oh yes,' Johanna replied indifferently, 'it will have been his heart, I suppose. The doctor lives thirty miles away and is drunk; he will come in the morning. Why do you eat so little? You should take more exercise. I will lend you a mare in the morning, a gallop will do you good.'

I became scarlet and silent.

The old lady rang a silver bell which stood by her place and a whey-faced priest stole in and said a long Latin grace to which both the women listened with bent heads. Then the Countess rose and made her way with fragile dignity to the door, where she let out a fart of such frightening power and timbre that I feared she had done herself a mischief. The priest sat down at the end of the table and began gobbling nuts and guzzling wine as though his life depended on it. Johanna sat smiling dreamily into space, presumably envisaging a blissfully Krampf-free future. I certainly hoped she was not envisaging any bliss which would involve my participation in the near future: all I wanted was some Scotch and a big fat sleeping pill.

It was not to be. Johanna took me by the hand and led me off to see the corpse, much as one might be taken to see the ornamental waterfowl in an English house. Krampf lay naked and nasty and very dead indeed, displaying all the signs of a massive coronary occlusion, as the thriller writers say. (There are *no* outward signs of death by massive coronary occlusion.) On the carpet beside his bed lay a little silver box which I remembered; it always held his heart pills. Krampf had gone to join Hockbottle: dicky tickers, both of them. To name but a few.

His death solved a few problems and created a few more. There was something about the situation which I could not, at that stage of the evening, quite define, but I knew that the word 'trouble' figured in it somewhere. Feeling sure that Johanna would not mind, I drew back the sheet which covered him: there was no mark of violence on his lardy body. She came and stood on the other side of the bed and we looked down at him dispassionately. I had lost a rich customer; she had lost a rich husband; there was little quantitative difference between our sorrows and the qualitative difference was that she, presumably, stood to gain a lot of money and I stood to lose some. Had Krampf been alive he would have felt like Jesus Christ between the two thieves, and indeed, death had lent him a certain spirituality, a certain waxy saintliness.

'He was a dirty ape,' she said at last. 'Also base and greedy.'

'I am all those things,' I answered quietly, 'yet I do not think I am like Krampf was.'

'No,' she said. 'He was mean in a shabby, tight-fisted way. I do not think you are mean like that, or at all. Why should rich men be mean?'

'I think it is because they would like to stay rich.'

She thought about that and didn't like it.

'No,' she said again. 'His greed was not of that sort. It was other people's lives he was greedy for: he collected his fellow men like postage stamps. He did not really want the stolen picture which you have in the cover of the Rolls Royce: it was you he was buying. You would never have got free from him after this deal.

You would have been kissing his pimply behind for the rest of your life.'

This upset me very much. First, even Krampf could not have known – should not have known – just where the Goya was supposed to be hidden; second, here was yet another person apparently manipulating me instead of *vice versa*; third, this was a woman, for God's sake, deep into the conspiracy and bubbling over with dangerous facts. Krampf had always been rash but he knew the basic rules of villainy. How on earth had he sunk to the point of telling things to a woman?

The whole complexion of Krampf's death changed; before, it had been an extreme awkwardness, now it was a peril. With all this dangerous knowledge surging about so freely there were dozens of motives for killing him when previously there had only been one: Martland's.

Moreover, I had decided only that morning not to carry out my part of the contract I had made with Martland for the terminating of Krampf. I have no patience with the absurd respect in which human life is held these days – indeed, our chief trouble is that there is far too *much* human life around – but as I grow older I find myself less and less keen on actually topping people myself. Particularly when they happen to be my best customers. Nevertheless, I should probably have kept faith with Martland as per contract had it not occurred to me that morning that I was already on the butcher's bill myself and that once I had killed Krampf I would be there redoubled, in spades, for a variety of reasons which you can surely work out for yourself.

'When did he go mad, child?' I asked gently.

'In the womb, I think. Badly, when he started to make plots with a man called Gloag.'

I winced.

'Yes,' I said, 'that figures.'

Despite appearances I was now certain that Krampf had been murdered: there were far too many motives. There are also far too many ways of simulating death by heart disease – and even more of inducing it in someone already prone to it.

I was piggy-in-the-middle and it felt horrid. Only Martland's word as a prefect stood between me and the ultimate in whackings from that fell school sergeant Death. Martland's word was as good as his bond, but his bond was mere Monopoly money. I pulled myself together.

'Well, Johanna,' I said brightly, 'I must be off to bed.'

'Yes,' she said, taking me firmly by the hand, 'we must.'

'Look, my dear, I'm really awfully tired, you know. And I'm not a young man any more . . .'

'Ah, but I have a way of curing both those things – come and see.'

I'm not really weak, you know, just bad and easily led. I shambled after her, my manhood cringing. The night was intolerably hot.

Her room greeted us with steamy heat like a buffet in the face – I panicked as she drew me in and bolted the door.

'The windows are sealed,' she explained, 'the drapes are closed, the central heating turned up high. Look, I am sweating already!'

I looked. She was.

'This is the best way of all to do it,' she went on, peeling off my drenched shirt, 'and you will find yourself young and vigorous, I promise you, it never fails, we shall be like animals in a tropical swamp.

I tried a tentative bellow of lust but without much conviction. She was anointing me copiously from a bottle of baby oil, handing me the bottle, stepping out of the last of her clothes and offering the astonishing landscape of her steaming body to the oil. I oiled. From some undreamed-of reservoir my body summoned up a gravity tank of incalescent libido.

'There, you see?' she said, gaily, pointing at me, and led me to one of those terrifying water-filled plastic beds – eclipsing me with her deliquescent body, coaxing succulent sounds from the contiguity of our bellies, shaming forth a long dead, steel hard, adolescent Mortdecai demented with furtive lust: Mortdecai Minor, the likeliest candidate for wanker's doom.

'Tonight, because you are tired, I am no longer the mare. You are the lazy circus horse and I shall school you in the *haute école*. Lie back, you will like this very much, I promise.'

I liked it.

14

OTTIMA: Then, Venus' body, had we come upon
    My husband Luca Gaddi's murdered corpse
    Within there, at his couch-foot, covered close –
    Would you have pored upon it? Why persist
    In poring now upon it? . . .

SEBALD: Off, off; take your hands off mine!
    'Tis the hot evening – off! Oh, morning, is it?
                             Pippa Passes

Slowly, painfully, I ungummed my eyes. The room was still in utter blackness and smelled of goat. A clock had been chiming somewhere but what hour, of what day even, I knew not. I suppose you could say that I had slept fitfully but I cannot pretend that I awoke refreshed. More knackered, really. I squirmed out of the steaming bed and dragged myself wetly to where the window had to be. I was one hundred years old and knew that my prostate gland could never be the same again. What I panted for, as the hart for cooling springs, was fresh air – not a commodity I often pant for. I found the heavy drapes, drew them apart with an effort and reeled back aghast. Outside, a carnival was in full swing – I thought I had taken leave of my senses, despite prep school assurances that you go *blind* first.

The windows on this side of the house gave on to the desert and there, a couple of furlongs from the house, the darkness was splashed with crisscross rows of coloured lights, blazing for half a mile in each direction. As I gaped uncomprehendingly Johanna slithered up behind me and pasted her viscous form lovingly against my back.

'They have lit up the airstrip, little stallion,' she murmured soothingly between my shoulder blades, 'a plane must be arriving. I wonder who?' What she was really wondering, evidently, was whether spavined old Mortdecai had one more gallop left in his thoroughbred loins but the sheepish answer was plain to see. Her loving moo became a *moue* but she did not reproach me. She was a *lady* – I know it sounds silly – still is for all I know.

Effete or not, I have strong feelings about aircraft landing unexpectedly in the early hours of the morning at country houses where I am staying in equivocal circumstances. It is my invariable practice in such cases to greet the occupants of these machines fully dressed, showered and with a pistol or similar device in my waistband, lest they (the aviators) should prove to be inimical to my best interests.

Accordingly, I showered, dressed, tucked the Banker's Special into its cosy nest and made for the great downstairs, where I found something astonishingly nasty to drink called *tequila*. It tasted of fine old vintage battery acid but I drank quite a lot of it, thirstily, before Johanna came down. She looked courteous, friendly but aloof; no hint of our late chumminess apparent on her lovely face.

A peon fluttered in and harangued her in the vile *argot* which passes for Spanish in those parts. She turned to me, well-bred surprise civilly concealed.

'A Señor Strapp has arrived,' she said wonderingly, 'and says that he must see you at once. He says that you expect him . . . ?'

I boggled a moment, about to deny all knowledge of any Strapps, before the penny dropped and the mental W.C. door flew open.

'Ah, yes, of course,' I cried, 'that's old Jock! Quite forgotten. Silly of me. My servant, sort of. Should have told you he was meeting me here. He'll really be no trouble, just a heap of bedding and a bone to gnaw. Should have warned you. Sorry.'

Even as I babbled, Jock's massy frame filled the doorway, his ill-hewn ashlar head weaving from side to side, eyes blinking at the light. I gave a glad cry and he returned a one-fang grin.

'Jock!' I cried, 'I am so glad you could come.' (Johanna, inexplicably, giggled.) 'I trust you are well, Jock and, er, *fit?*' He caught my drift and blinked affirmatively. 'Go and get washed and fed, Jock, then meet me here, please, in half an hour. We are leaving.'

He shambled off, led by a she-peon, and Johanna rounded on me.

'How can you be leaving? Do you not love me? What have I done? Are we not to be married?' This was my day for gaping – I did it again. While I gaped she continued her amazing tirade.

'Do you think I give myself like an animal to every man I meet? Did you not realize last night that you are my first and only passion, that I belong to you, that I am your woman?'

Huckleberry Finn's words sprang to my mind: 'The statements was interesting but tough,' but this was no time for breezy quoting – she looked as though one wrong answer would send her galloping up to the boudoir for her Dragoon Colts. My jaws unlocked themselves and I began to drivel fast, as though drivelling for my life.

'Never dreamed . . . didn't dare hope . . . plaything of an idle hour . . . too old . . . too fat . . . burned out . . . bemused . . . haven't had my tea . . . in terrible danger here . . .' That last bit seemed to interest her: I had to give a clumsily edited version of my grounds for fear; such as Martlands, Buicks, Bluchers and Brauns, to name but a few.

'I see,' she said at last. 'Yes, in the circumstances perhaps you had better leave for the moment. When you are safe, get in touch with me and I will come to you and we shall be happy ever after. Take the Rolls Royce – and anything in it – it is my engagement present to you.'

'Good God,' I quavered, aghast, 'you can't give me that, I mean, worth a fortune, quite ridiculous.'

'I already have a fortune,' she said, simply. 'Also, I love you. Please not to insult me by refusing. Try to understand that I am yours and so, naturally, everything I have is yours too.'

'Gaw Blimey,' I thought. Clearly, I was being ridiculed in some complicated way – and for unguessed-at reasons – or was I? The glint in her eye was dangerous, genuinely.

'Ah, well, in that case,' I said, 'there is one thing I really have to have for my own safety – it's a sort of photographic negative, I fancy, and perhaps some prints of – well –'

'Of two deviates playing at bulldozers? I know it. The faces have been cut out of the print but my husband says that one of them is the nasty Mr Gloag and the other the brother-in-law of your –'

'Yes, yes,' I broke in. 'That's it. The very thing. No use to you, you know. Your husband was only going to use it to get diplomatic bag facilities for stolen pictures and even that was too dangerous. Even for him. I mean, look at him.'

She looked at *me* curiously for a while then led the way to Krampf's study, which was a riot of undigested wealth, a cinema usherette's nightmare of Tsarskoe Selo. When I tell you that the central attraction – the Main Feature, so to speak – was an enormous, nude, hairy trollop by Henner which hung against Louis XIV *boiseries* and was lit by two of the most awful Tiffany lamps I have ever seen, then I think I have said all. Mrs Spon would have *catted* right there, on the Aubusson.

'*Merde*,' I said, awestruck.

She nodded gravely. 'It is beautiful, is it not. I designed it for him when we were first married, when I still thought I loved him.'

She led the way through Krampf's private bog, where a fine Bouguereau – if you like Bouguereau – twinkled saucy titties and bums down into the still waters of a porcelain *bidet* which might have been designed for Catherine the Great in one of her more salty moods. The picture, cunningly, did not conceal a safe, but a carved panel just beside it did. Johanna had to diddle it in all sorts of complicated ways before it swung open to reveal groaning shelves of great coarse currency notes – I've never seen such a vulgar sight – as well as passbooks from the banks of all the world and a number of leather-covered suitcase handles. (I did not have to heft these to know that they were made of platinum, for I had given Krampf the notion myself. It's a good wheeze, the customs haven't got on to it yet. You're welcome, I shan't need it again.) She opened a drawer concealed in the side wall of the safe and tossed a parcel of envelopes to me.

'What you want should be in there,' she said indifferently and went to perch delicately on the edge of the bidet. I riffled through the package reverently. One envelope contained insurance policies beyond the dreams of avarice, another a mass of wills and codicils, another held simply a list of names with coded references against each. (Knowing Krampf's predilections, there was probably a fortune in that list alone, if one spent a little time on it, but I am not a brave man.) The next envelope was full of smaller envelopes, each one bearing a rare foreign stamp in the top right-hand corner: rich and devious readers will recognize the dodge – you simply stick an ordinary new postage stamp over the rarity and post it to yourself or your agent in some foreign capital. It is the easiest way of moving heavy spending money about the world without losing too much in commission.

The last envelope was the one I wanted – needed – and it seemed to be in order. There was the magnum print with the faces cut out and a strip of 35-mm negatives on British film stock. A length of amateurish contact prints mostly showed the Backs at Cambridge but the centre frame showed the fronts all right: Hockbottle seemed to have been in charge that day and it had been Chummy's turn in the barrel. His familiar grin, straight into the camera, showed that he didn't mind a bit. I burned it without compunction and threw the ashes into the naughty *bidet*. It represented a lot of money but, as I just said, I am not a brave man – even money can come too dear.

I was not troubled about the possible existence of other prints: Krampf may have been imprudent but he had nor, I thought, been wholly potty and, in any case, prints are too easily faked these days; people want to see the negative – and the original negative at that, negatives prepared from a positive print are easily detectable.

She twisted round and stared at the smear of ashes in the *bidet*.

'Are you happy now, Charlie? Is that really all you wanted?'

'Yes. Thank you. It makes me a little safer, I think. Not much, but a little. Thank you very much.'

She rose and went to the safe, selected a couple of chunks of currency and closed the panel negligently.

'Here is some journey money, please take it. You will perhaps need *des fonds sérieux* to help you get safely away.'

They were two fat bricks of bank notes, still in their wrappers, one English, one American. The total amount had to be something quite indecent.

'Oh, but I couldn't possibly take this,' I squeaked, 'it's a terrible lot of money.'

'But I keep telling you, I *have* a terrible lot of money now – this in the safe is nothing, a cash reserve he kept for small bribes to Senators and for unexpected trips. You are please to take it; I shall not be happy unless I know that you have proper funds while you are avoiding these unpleasant men.'

My further protestations were cut short by frightful shrieks from downstairs, superimposed on a bass of snarling roars. We raced for the stairhead and looked down into the hall on a scene of gladiatorial horror: Jock had a peon in each hand and was methodically beating them together like a pair of cymbals, while others, of both sexes, milled around him, tore at his hair, hung on his arms and were hurled off spinning across the tiled floor.

'¡Bravo toro!' cried Johanna piercingly and the mêlée became a tableau.

'Put those people down, Jock,' I said severely, 'you don't know where they've been.'

'I was only trying to find out what they'd done with you, Mr Charlie – you said half an hour, didn't you?'

I apologized all round; the peons couldn't understand my polished Castilian but they knew what it was all right; there was a good deal of bowing and scraping and forelock-tugging and polite murmurs of 'de nada' and they accepted a dollar apiece with every mark of pleasure. One went so far as to intimate courteously that, since his nose was squashed to a pulp, he merited a little extra honorarium but Johanna would not let me give him any more.

'With one dollar he will get beautifully drunk,' she explained, 'but with two he would do something foolish, perhaps go off and get married.'

She explained this to the peon, too, who followed her reasoning carefully and gravely concurred at the end. They are a logical lot.

'A logical lot, Jock, don't you think?' I asked later.

'Nah,' he said. 'Lot of bloody Pakis if you ask me.'

We got away before the sun was very high. I had breakfasted lightly on a little more tequila – it's beastly but it sort of grows on you – and had contrived to avoid a farewell exhibition-bout with my doting Johanna. She was most convincingly tearful and distrait, saying that she would live only for my message that she might join me and live happily ever after.

'Where we going, then, Mr Charlie?'

'I'll think about that as we go, Jock. In the meantime, there's only this road. Let's move.'

But as we drove – as Jock drove, to be exact, for he had slept on the plane – I mused about Johanna. What earthly purpose could all that incredible codswallop of hers be serving? Did she really think that I was swallowing it? Did she think I could believe her bowled over by the faded allure of portly, past-it Mortdecai? 'Gain' was the word which kept springing to mind. And yet; and yet . . . Karl Popper urges us to be constantly on our guard against the fashionable disease of our time: the assumption that things cannot be taken at their face value, that an apparent syllogism must be the *rationale* of an irrational motive, that a human avowal must conceal some self-seeking baseness. (Freud assures us that Leonardo's John the Baptist is a homosexual symbol, his upward-pointing index finger seeking to penetrate the fundament of the universe; art historians know that it is a centuries-old cliché of Christian iconography.)

Perhaps, then, all was as it seemed, all to the gravy; indeed, as we soared up winding roads into the high country stretching its strong limbs in the young sunshine, it was hard to credit my fears and suspicions.

Perhaps Krampf had indeed died of heart disease after excess at table: statistically he was a sitter for just that. Perhaps Johanna had indeed fallen violently in love with me: my friends have sometimes been kind enough to say that I have a certain appeal, perhaps an adroitness in these little matters. Perhaps the second powder-blue Buick and its driver were merely a relief shift ordered by Krampf: I had had no opportunity to put this to him. Perhaps, last of all, I would indeed send for Johanna and live the life of Riley with her and her millions until my glands gave out.

The more I thought about this view of things the more sensible it became and the sweeter shone the sun on the unjust. I leaned back luxuriously into the rich-smelling leather of the Rolls – *my* Rolls! – and quietly whistled a happy stave or two.

Martland, surely, would never believe that Krampf's infarct was natural; he would assume that I had murdered him as per invoice and had been devilish clever about it.

Only Johanna knew that I had burned the negative and if I dropped the merest hint to Martland that I might just have forgotten to do so he would never dare unleash his death dogs on me but would be forced to respect his word and protect me from all annoyances; such as, for instance, death.

I liked it; I liked it all, it fitted together, it made nonsense of my fears, I felt positively young again. For two pins, I'd have turned back and given Johanna a little farewell token of my esteem after all, that's how young I felt. The lark was on the wing and flying strongly, while the snail was positively striding up its favourite thorn.

Admittedly, there was one fly trampling about in the ointment of my content: I was now the proud but shy owner of about half a million pounds' worth of hot Goya – the hottest piece of property in the world. Despite what you read in the Sunday papers, America is not seething with mad millionaires panting to buy stolen masterpieces and gloat over them in their underground aviaries. As a matter of fact, the late Krampf had been the only one I knew of and I did not much want another like him. A superb spender, but hard on the nervous system.

Destroying the painting was out of the question: my soul is all stained and shagged with sin like a cigarette smoker's moustache but I am quite incapable of destroying works of art. Steal them, yes, cheerfully, it is a mark of respect and love, but destroy them, never. Why, even the Woosters had a code, as we are told on the highest authority.

Probably the best thing was to take it back to England – it was, after all, as well hidden now as it ever could be – and get in touch with a specialist friend who knows how to do discreet deals with insurance companies.

You know, all those dreary pink Renoirs which are incessantly getting pinched in the South of France are either sold back to the insurers at a straight 20 per cent of the sum insured – the companies won't pay a franc more, it's a matter of professional ethics – or they are pinched at the express request of the owners and immediately destroyed. The French *arriviste,* you see, lives in such a continual agony of snobbism that he dares not put his Renoir, bought three

years ago, into a public auction and so admit that he is short of a little change – still less dare he take the risk that it might fetch less than
he has told all his awful friends it is worth. He would rather die; or,
in practical terms, he would rather assassinate the painting and collect
the *nouveaux francs*. In England the police tend to purse their lips and
wag their fingers at insurance co's who buy back stolen things from
the thieves: they feel that this is not a way to discourage villainy – in
fact the whole process is strictly against the law.

Nevertheless, if a certain young man, not unknown at Lloyd's,
murmurs in the proper ear that a bundle of currency posted to an
accommodation address in Streatham will bring about a change of heart
in certain thieves and cause them to panic and dump the swag in a left-
luggage office – well, insurance co's are only human you know (or
didn't you know?) and a thousand pounds is a great deal less than, say,
five thousand ditto. The certain young man not unknown at Lloyd's
was also not unknown to me and although he didn't like murmuring in
that sort of ear more than once or twice a year he had, I knew, a heart
of gold and owed me a trifling kindness. Moreover, he was terrified of
Jock. Don't think I'm recommending this particular caper, though: the
police are professionals and we laymen are only gifted amateurs, at the
best. If you must sin, find an obscure, unexplored branch of crime that
the Yard hasn't any experts in and work it gently, don't milk it dry, and
vary your *modus operandi* continually. They'll get on to you in the end,
of course, but if you're not greedy you may have a few good years first.

As I was saying, before the above gnomic utterances, I was by
now wholly reconciled to a Panglossian view of things: all was expli-
cable, the tangled web made, after all, a comprehensible pattern when
looked at in sunlight and also, after all, one Mortdecai was worth a
whole barrelful of Martlands, Bluchers, Krampfs and other dullards.
('One of the most remarkable phenomena connected with the practice
of mendacity is the vast number of deliberate lies we tell ourselves,
whom, of all persons, we can least expect to deceive.' J.S. Lefanu.)

To complete my skimpy breakfast, and to celebrate the victory of
virtue over dullness, I opened a bottle of the twelve-year-old Scotch
and was just raising it to my lips when I saw the powder-blue Buick.
It was coming out of an *arroyo* ahead of us, coming fast, engine howl-

ing in a low gear, coming straight for our nearside. Our offside was
barely a yard from a sheer drop of hundreds of feet – it was a fair cop.
I'd had my life. Jock – I've told you how fast he could be when necessary – wrenched the wheel over to the left, stood on the brakes,
snatched first gear before the Rolls stalled and was turning right as
the Buick hit us. The Buick man had known nothing of the strength
of a vintage Rolls Royce, nor of Jock's fighting brain; our radiator
gutted his car's side with a ghastly shriek of metal and the Buick span
like a top, ending up poised on the shoulder of the road, its rear end
impossibly extended over the precipice. The driver, face contorted
with who knows what emotion, was fighting frantically with the door
handle, his features a mask of nasty blood. Jock got out, ponderously
strolled over to him and stared, looked up and down the road, went to
the front of the mangled Buick, found a handhold and heaved enormously. The Buick tilted, started to go very slowly: Jock had time to
get to the window again and give the driver a friendly grin before the
nose went up and slid out of sight, slowly still. The driver showed us
all his teeth in a silent scream before he went; we heard the Buick
bounce three times, amazingly loudly, but never a thread of the driver's scream – those Buicks must be better soundproofed than you'd
think. I believe, but I am not sure even now, that it was friendly Mr
Braun – who was once again proving to me the statistical improbability of death in an aircraft accident.

I was surprised – and pardonably proud – to find that throughout
the episode I had not lost my grip on the Scotch bottle: I had my drink
and, since the circumstances were exceptional, offered the bottle to
Jock.

'That was a bit vindictive, Jock,' I said reprovingly.

'Lost my temper,' he admitted. 'Bloody road hog.'

'He might easily have done us a mischief,' I agreed. Then I told
him about things, especially like powder-blue Buicks and the dreadful – is that word really so worn out? – the dreadful danger I was –
we were – in, despite my recent brief and lovely courtship with the
phantasms of success, safety and happy-ever-after. (It seemed hard to
believe that I could have been dallying, so few minutes before, with
so patently tinsel a mental mistress as safety.) My eloquence ran to

such heights of bitter self-mockery that I heard myself, aghast, telling Jock to leave me, to get out from under before the great axe fell.

'Bollocks,' I'm happy to say, was his response to that suggestion. (But 'happy to say' is not true either: his loyalty served me but briefly and him but shabbily – you might say that his 'bollocks' were the death of him.)

When the whisky had somewhat soothed our nerves we corked the bottle and got out of the car to examine its wounds. An Anglia driver would have done this first, of course, raging at fate, but we Rolls owners are made of sterner stuff. The radiator was scarred, weeping a little on to the baking road; a headlamp and sidelamp were quite ruined; the offside mudguard was heavily crumpled but still not quite so much that it would flay the tire. The show was, if necessary, on the road. I went back into the car and thought, while Jock fussed over the damage. I may have sipped a little at the whisky bottle and who shall blame me?

No one passed along the road, in either direction. A grasshopper stridulated endlessly; I minded this at first but soon learned to live with it. Having thought, I checked my thinking both ways from the ace. The result came out the same again and again. I didn't like it, but there you are, aren't you?

We sent the Rolls over the precipice. I am not ashamed to say that I wept a little to see all that beauty, that power and grace and history, being tossed into an arid canyon like a cigar end chucked down a lavatory pan. Even in death the car was elegant; it described great majestic curves as it rebounded in an almost leisurely way from boulder to boulder and came to rest, far below us, wedged upside-down in the throat of a deep crevasse, its lovely underparts bared to the sex of sunshine for a few seconds before a hundred tons of scree, dislodged by its passage, roared down and covered it.

The death of the Buick driver had been nothing compared with this: human death in reality seems poor stuff to a devoted television watcher, but who amongst you, seasoned readers, has seen a Rolls Royce Silver Ghost die on its back? I was inexpressibly moved. Jock seemed to sense this in his rough way for he moved closer to me and uttered words of comfort.

'It was insured full comprehensive, Mr Charlie,' he said.

'Yes, Jock,' I answered gruffly, 'you read my thoughts, as usual. But what is more to the point, just now, is how easily could the Rolls be salvaged?'

He brooded down into the shimmering, rock-strewn haze.

'How are you getting down there?' he began. 'This side's all avalanches and the other side's a cliff. Very dodgy.'

'Right.'

'Then you got to get it out of that crack, haven't you?'

'Right again.'

'*Dead* dodgy.'

'Yes.'

'And then you got to get it back up here, right?'

'Right.'

'Have to close this road a couple of days while the tackle's working, I reckon.'

'That's what I thought.'

'Mind you, if it was some stupid mountaineering twit stuck down there, or some old tart's puppy dog, they'd have him up before you could cough, wouldn't they, but this is only an old jam jar, isn't it? You'd have to want it real bad – or want something in it real bad – before you'd go slummocking down there.' He nudged me and winked enormously. He was never very good at winking, it contorted his face horribly. I nudged him back. We smirked.

Then we trudged up the road, Jock carrying our one suitcase now holding essentials for both of us, which he was supposed to have salvaged with wonderful presence of mind as the Rolls teetered on the very brink of the precipice.

'Whither Mortdecai?' about summed up my thought on that baking, dusty road. It is hard to think constructively once the fine, white grit of New Mexico has crept up your trouser legs and joined the sweat of your crotch. All I could decide was that the stars in their courses were hotly anti-Mortdecai and that, noble sentiments aside, I was well rid of what was probably the most conspicuous motor car on the North American subcontinent.

On the other hand, pedestrians are more conspicuous in New

Mexico than most motor cars: a fact I realized when a car swept past us going in the direction we had come from; all its occupants goggled at us as though we were Teenage Things from Outer Space. It was an official car of some sort, a black and white Olds-mobile Super 88, and it did not stop – why should it? To be on foot in the United States is only immoral, not illegal. Unless you're a bum, of course. It's just like in England, really: you can wander abroad and lodge in the open air so long as you've a home to go to; it's only an offence if you *haven't* one – on the same principle that ensures you cannot borrow money from a bank unless you don't need any.

After what seemed a great many hours we found a patch of shade afforded by some nameless starveling trees and without a word spoken we sank down in their ungenerous umbrage.

'When a car passes going in our direction, Jock, we shall leap to our feet and hail it.'

'All right, Mr Charlie.'

With that we both fell asleep instantly.

15

John of the Temple, whose fame so bragged.
Is burning alive in Paris square!
How can he curse, if his mouth is gagged?
Or wriggle his neck, with a collar there?
Or heave his chest, while a band goes round?
Or threat with his fist, since his arms are spliced?
Or kick with his feet, now his legs are bound?
– Thinks John, I will call upon Jesus Christ.
The Heretic's Tragedy

A couple of hours later we were rudely awakened when a car travel-
ling in our direction screeched to a halt beside us. It was the official
looking car which had passed earlier and four huge rough men poured
out of it, waving pistols and handcuffs and other symbols of Law 'n'
Order. In a trice, before we were properly awake, we were sitting
manacled in the car, surrounded by deputy sheriffs. Jock, when he had
sized up the situation, started to make a deep growling noise and to
tense his muscles. The deputy beside him, with a deft backhanded
flip, laid a leather-covered blackjack smartly against Jock's upper lip
and nostrils. It is exquisitely painful: tears sprang to Jock's eyes and
he fell silent.

'Now look here!' I cried angrily.

'Shaddap.'

I too fell silent.

They hit Jock again when we arrived at the sheriff's office in the
single broad dusty street of an empty little town; he had shrugged off
the deputy's officious hands and made snarling noises, so one of them
casually bent down and cashed him hard behind the knee. That is
pretty painful too; we all had to wait a while before he could walk into

the office – he was much too big to carry. They didn't hit me; I was *demure*.

What they do to you in this particular sheriff's office is as follows: they hang you up on a door by your handcuffs then they hit you quite gently but insistently on the kidneys, for quite a long time. It makes you cry, if you want to know. It would make anybody cry after a time. They don't ask you any questions and they don't leave any marks on you, except where the handcuffs bit in, and you did that yourself, struggling, didn't you?

'*I shut my eyes and turned them on my heart, I asked one draught of earlier, happier sights* . . .'

After a certain time the sheriff himself came into the room. He was a slight and studious man with an intelligent look and a disapproving scowl. The deputies stopped hitting our kidneys and pocketed their blackjacks.

'Why have these men not been charged?' he asked coldly. 'How many times do I have to tell you that suspects are not to be questioned before they have been properly booked?'

'We weren't questioning them, sheriff,' said one in an insubordinate tone. 'If we was questioning them they'd be hanging the other way around and we'd be beating on their balls, you know that, sheriff. We was just kind of getting their minds right for being questioned by *you*, sheriff.'

He stroked his face all down one side, quite thoroughly, making a gentle, half-audible sound like an old lady caressing a pet toad.

'Bring them in to me,' he said and turned on his heel.

'Bring' was right – we couldn't have made our own way to his office. He let us sit on chairs, but only because we couldn't stand up. Now, suddenly, I was very angry indeed, a rare emotion for me and one which I have schooled myself to avoid since my disastrous childhood.

When I could speak properly through the choking and the sobs I gave him the full business, especially the diplomatic passport bit. It worked, he started to look angry himself and perhaps a little frightened. Our gyves were removed and our possessions returned to us, except for my Banker's Special. Jock's Luger was in the suitcase

which, I was relieved to notice, had not been opened: Jock had pru-
dently swallowed the key and, in the excitement of spoiling our personal plumbing, the deputies had not taken time out to force the lock.
It was a very *good* lock and a very strong case.

'Now you will have the goodness, perhaps, to explain this
extraordinary treatment, Sir,' I said, giving him my dirtiest glare, 'and
suggest reasons why I should not request my Ambassador to arrange
to have you and your ruffians broken.'

He looked at me long and thoughtfully, his clever eyes flickering
as his brain raced. I was a lot of trouble for him whichever way the
cat jumped; a lot of paperwork at the best, a lot of grief at the worst.
I could see him reach a decision and I trembled inwardly. Before he
could speak I attacked again.

'If you choose not to answer, of course, I can simply call the
embassy and give them the bald facts as they stand.'

'Don't push too hard, Mr Mortdecai. I am about to book you both
on suspicion of murder and your diplomatic status isn't worth a pile
of rat dirt in that league.'

I spluttered in a British sort of way to hide my consternation.
Surely no one could have seen Jock's little momentary squib of ill-
temper with the Buick – and anyway, at a distance it would surely
have seemed that he was trying to *save* the poor fellow . . .?

'Just who am I – are we – supposed to have murdered?'

'Milton Quintus Desiré Krampf.'

'*Desiré?*'

'That's how I have it.'

'Gawblimey. You're sure it wasn't *'Voulu?'*

'No,' he said, in a literate sort of way and with half a smile.
'"Desiré" is how I have it here.' One got the impression that if he'd
been an Englishman he'd have seconded my 'Gawblimey' but one
had, too, the impression that he was quite content *not* to be an
Englishman, perhaps particularly not the portly Englishman now
cowering manfully in front of him.

'Go on,' I said. 'Frighten me.'

'I never try to. Some people I hurt; it's part of the job. Some I kill:
that too. Who needs to frighten? I'm not that kind of a policeman.'

'I bet you frighten your psychiatrist,' I quipped and straightaway wished I hadn't. He did not give me a cold, blank stare, he didn't look at me at all. He looked at the desk top where the scratches and the fly shit were, then he opened a drawer and took out one of those thin, black, gnarled cheroots and lit it. He didn't even blow the rank smoke in my face – he wasn't that kind of a policeman.

But he had, somehow, succeeded in frightening me. My kidneys started to hurt terribly.

'My kidneys are hurting me terribly,' I said, 'and I have to go to the lavatory.'

He gestured economically toward a door and I got there without actually screaming out loud. It was a very *nice* little lavatory. I rested my head against the cool, tiled wall and piddled wearily. There was no actual blood, which mildly surprised me. At eye level someone had scratched 'MOTHER F' into the wall before they had been interrupted. I speculated – '– ATHER'? – then collected myself, remembering Jock's plight; adjusted clothing before leaving.

'Your turn, Jock,' I said firmly as I re-entered the room, 'should have thought of you first.' Jock shambled out; the sheriff didn't look impatient, he didn't really look anything – I wished he would. I cleared my throat.

'Sheriff,' I said, 'I saw Mr Krampf's body yesterday – goodness, was it only yesterday – and he had quite clearly died of a coronary in the ordinary way of business. What gives with the murder bit?'

'You may speak English, Mr Mortdecai; I am an uneducated man but I read a great deal. Mr Krampf died of a deep puncture wound in the heart. Someone – you, I must suppose – introduced a long and very thin instrument into his side between the fifth and sixth ribs and carefully wiped off the very slight surface bleeding which would have ensued.

'It is not a rare *modus operandi* on our West Coast: the Chinese Tongs used to favour a six-inch nail, the Japanese use a sharpened umbrella rib. It's all-same Sicilian stiletto, I suppose, except that the Sicilians usually strike upwards through the diaphragm. Had Mr Krampf's heart been young and sound he might well have survived so small a puncture – the muscle could have kind of clenched itself around the hole – but Mr Krampf's heart was by no means healthy. Had he been a poor man his history of heart disease might have caused the manner of his death to escape notice, but he was not a man at all, he was a hundred million dollars. That means a great deal of insurance pressure in this country, Mr Mortdecai, and our insurance investigators make the Chicago riot police look like Girl Scouts. Even the drunkest doctor takes a veddy, veddy careful look at a hundred million dollars' worth of dead meat.'

I pondered a bit. Dawn broke.

'The old lady!' I cried. 'The Countess! A hatpin! She was a leading Krampf-hater and a hatpin owner if ever I saw one!'

He shook his head slowly. 'Not a chance, Mr Mortdecai. I'm surprised to hear you trying to pin your slaying on the sweetest and innocentest little old lady you ever saw. Besides, we already checked. She covers her head with a shawl in church and doesn't have a hat or a hatpin in her possession. We *looked*. Anyway, one of the servants has sworn a statement that you were seen entering Krampf's personal suite, drunk, at about the time of death and that your servant Strapp acted like a homicidal maniac during your visit to the rancho, breaking the same servant's nose and beating up everyone. Moreover, you are known to be Mrs Krampf's lover – we have a really fascinating statement from the woman who makes her bed – so there's a double motive of sex and money as well as opportunity. I'd say you should tell it all now, starting with where you hid the murder weapon, so I don't have to have you interrogated.'

He repeated the word 'interrogated' as though he liked the sound of it. To say that my blood ran cold would be idle: it was already as cold as a tart's kiss. Had I been guilty I would have 'spilled my guts' – may I use dialect? – there and then, rather than meet those deputies again, especially *frontally*. If Winter comes, can Spring be far behind? A still, small voice whispered 'stall' in my ear.

'Do you mean to say that you have arrested Johanna Krampf?' I cried.

'Mr Mortdecai, you cannot be as simple as you pretend. Mrs Krampf is now many millions of dollars herself; a poor sheriff does not arrest millions of dollars, they have not a stain on their character.

Should I call in a stenographer now, so that you can make the statement?'

What had I to lose? In any case, no one could hurt me too obscenely in front of a sweet little bosomy stenographer.

So he pressed a buzzer and in clunked the nastier of the two deputies, a pencil engulfed in one meaty fist, a shorthand pad in the other.

I may have squeaked – I don't remember and it is not important. There is no doubt that I was distressed.

'Are you unwell, Mr Mortdecai?' asked the sheriff pleasantly.

'Not really,' I said. 'Just a touch of proctalgia.' He didn't ask what it meant; just as well, really.

'Statement by C. Mortdecai,' he said crisply to the stenographic ruffian, 'given at so and so on such and such a date before me, so and so, and witnessed by such and such another.' With that he shot a finger out at me, like one of those capable television chaps. I did not hesitate: it was time to put on a bit of dog.

'I did not kill Krampf,' I said, 'and I have no idea who did. I am a British diplomat and protest strongly against this disgraceful treatment. I suggest you either release me at once or allow me to telephone the nearest British Consul before you ruin your career irretrievably. Can you spell "irretrievably"?' I asked over my shoulder at the stenographer. But he was no longer taking down my words, he was advancing toward me with the blackjack in his hairy paw. Before I could even cringe the door opened and two almost identical men entered.

This final Kafkaesque touch was too much for me: I succumbed to hysterical giggles. No one looked at me; the deputy was slinking out, the sheriff was looking at the two men's credentials, the two men were looking through the sheriff. Then the sheriff slunk out. I pulled myself together.

'What is the meaning of this intrusion?' I asked, still giggling like a little mad thing. They were very polite, pretended not to hear me, sat down side by side behind the sheriff's desk. They were astonishingly alike; the same suits, the same haircuts, the same neat briefcases and the same slight bulges under the nattily tailored left armpits.

They looked like Colonel Blucher's younger brothers. They were probably rather alarming people in their quiet way. I pulled myself together and stopped giggling. I could tell Jock didn't like them, he had started breathing through his nose, a sure sign.

One of them pulled out a little wire recorder, tested it briefly, switched it off and sat back, folding his arms. The other pulled out a slim manila file, read the contents with mild interest and sat back, folding his arms. They didn't look at each other once, they didn't look at Jock. First they looked at the ceiling for a while, as though it was something of a novelty, then they looked at me as though I was nothing of the kind. They looked at me as though they saw a great many of me every day and felt none the richer for it. One of them, on some unseen cue, at last uttered,

'Mr Mortdecai, we are members of a small Federal Agency of which you have never heard. We report directly to the Vice-President. We are in a position to help you. We have formed the opinion that you are in urgent need of help and we may say that this opinion has been formed after same extensive study of your recent activities, which seem to have been dumb.'

'Oh, ah,' I said feebly.

'I should make it very clear that we are not interested in law enforcement as such; indeed, such an interest would often conflict with our specific duties.'

'Yes,' I said. 'Do you know a chap called Colonel Blucher? Or, if it comes to that, another chap named Martland?'

'Mr Mortdecai, we feel we can best help you at this juncture by encouraging you to answer our questions rather than ask any of your own. A few right answers could get you out of here in ten minutes; wrong answers, or a whole lot of questions, would make us lose interest in you and we'd just kind of hand you back to the sheriff. Personally, and off the record, I would not, myself, care to be held for murder in this county, would you, Smith?'

Smith shook his head emphatically, lips tightened.

'Ask away,' I quavered, 'I have nothing to hide.'

'Well, that's already being a little less than candid, Sir, but we'll let it pass this time. Would you tell us first, please, what you did with

the negative and prints of a certain photograph, formerly in the possession of Milton Krampf?'

(Did you know that in the olden days when a sailor died at sea
and the sailmaker was sewing him up in his tarpaulin jacket, along
with an anchor shackle, prior to committing him to the deep, that the
last stitch was always ritually passed through the corpse's nose? It
was to give him his last chance to come to life and cry out. I felt like
just such a sailor at that moment. I came to life and cried out. This last
stitch had finally awakened me from the cataleptic trance I must have
been in for days. Far, far too many people knew far, far too much
about my little affairs: the game was up, all was known, God was not
in his heaven, the snail was unthorned and C. Mortdecai was *dans la
purée noire*. He had been *dumb*.)

'What negative?' I asked brightly.

They looked at each other wearily and began to gather their
things together. I was still being dumb.

'Wait!' I cried. 'Silly of me. The negative. Yes, of course. The
photographic negative. Yes. Oh, yes, yes, yes. As a matter of fact I
burned it, much too dangerous to have about one.'

'We are glad you said that, Sir, for we have reason to believe it
is true. Indeed, we found traces of ash in a, uh, curious footbath in Mr
Krampf's private bathroom.'

You will agree, I'm sure, that this was no time to expatiate on the
niceties of French plumbing.

'Well, there you are, you see,' I said.

'How many prints, Mr Mortdecai?'

'I burned the two with the negative; I only know of one other, in
London, and the faces have been cut out of that – I daresay you know
all about it.'

'Thank you. We feared you might pretend to know of others and
attempt to use this as a means of protecting yourself. It would not
have protected you but it would have given us a fair amount of embarrassment.'

'Oh, good.'

'Mr Mortdecai, have you asked yourself how we happen to be
here so soon after the killing?'

'Look, I said I'd answer your questions and I will: if I have guts I'm prepared to spill them now – I'm quite unmanned. But if you want me to ask *myself* questions, you must get me something to eat and drink. Anything will do to eat; my drink is in the outer office if King Kong and Godzilla out there haven't stolen it all. Oh, and my servant needs something too, of course.'

One of them put his head out of the door and muttered; my whisky, not too depleted, appeared and I sucked hungrily at it, then passed it to Jock. The boys in the Brooks Bros suits didn't want any – they probably lived on iced water and tin tacks.

'No,' I resumed, 'I have not asked myself that. If I really started to ask myself about the events of the last thirty-six hours I should probably be forced to conclude that there is a world-wide anti-Mortdecai conspiracy. But tell me, if it will cheer you up.'

'We don't much want to tell you, Mr Mortdecai. We just wanted to hear what you would say. So far we like your answers. Now tell us about the way you lost the Rolls Royce.' At this point they switched the wire recorder on.

I told them frankly about the collision but altered the subsequent events a little, telling them lovely stories about Jock's gallant bid to save the Buick as it teetered on the brink; then how we had tried to back the Rolls on to the road, how the wheels had spun, the shoulder crumbled and the car gone to join the Buick.

'And your suitcase, Mr Mortdecai?'

'Brilliant presence of mind on the part of Jock – snatched it at the last moment.'

They switched off the recorder.

'We do not necessarily believe all or any of this, Mr Mortdecai, but again it happens to be the story we wanted. Now, have you anything else in your possession which you intended to deliver to Mr Krampf?'

'No. Honour bright. *Search* us.'

They started studying the ceiling again, they had all the time in the world.

Later, the door knocked and a deputy brought in a paper sack of food; I almost fainted away at the wonderful fragrance of hamburgers and coffee. Jock and I ate two hamburgers each; our interrogators didn't like the look of theirs. They pushed them away delicately with the backs of their fingers, in unison, as though they'd rehearsed it. There was a little carton of chilli to spread on the hamburgers. I had lots of it but it spoils the taste of whisky, you know.

I cannot remember much about the rest of the questions, except that they went on for a long time and some of them were surprisingly vague and general. Sometimes the wire recorder was on, sometimes not. Probably another was on all the time, inside one of the briefcases. I got the impression that they were becoming very bored with the whole thing, but I was by then so sleepy with food and liquor and exhaustion that I could only concentrate with difficulty. Much of the time I simply told them the truth – a course Sir Henry Wotton (another man who went abroad to lie) recommended as a way of baffling your adversaries. Another chap once said, 'If you wish to preserve your secret, wrap it up in frankness.' I wrapped, profusely. But you know, playing a sort of fugue with truth and mendacity makes one lose, after a while, one's grip on reality. My father always warned me against lying where the truth would do; he had early realized that my memory – essential equipment of the liar – was faulty. 'Moreover,' he used to say, 'a lie is a work of art. We *sell* works of art, we don't give them away. Eschew falsehood, my son.' That is why I never lie when selling works of art. Buying them is another matter, of course.

As I was saying, they asked a lot of rather vague questions, few of them apparently germane to the issue. Mind you, I wasn't so terribly sure what the point at issue was, so perhaps I wasn't the best judge. They wanted to know about Hockbottle although they seemed to know more about him than I did. On the other hand, they seemed not to have heard that he was dead; funny, that. I brought Colonel Blucher's name into the conversation several times – I even tried pronouncing it 'Blootcher' – but they didn't react at all.

At last, they started stuffing their gear away into the matching briefcases with an air of finality, which warned me that the big question was about to be asked in an offhand, casual way as they rose to go.

'Tell me, Mr Mortdecai,' said one of them in an offhand, casual way as they rose to go, 'what did you think of Mrs Krampf?'

'Her heart,' I said bitterly, 'is like spittle on the palm that the Tartar slaps – no telling which way it will pitch.'

'That's very nice, Mr Mortdecai,' said one, nodding appreciatively, 'that's M.P. Shiel, isn't it? Do I understand that you consider her as being in some way responsible for your present predicament?'

'Of course I do, I'm not a complete bloody idiot. "Patsy" is the word over here, I believe.'

'You could just be mistaken there,' the other agent said gently. 'You have no cogent reason for supposing that Mrs Krampf is other than sincere in her feelings toward you; certainly none for supposing that she has set you up.'

I snarled.

'Mr. Mortdecai, I don't wish to be impertinent, but may I ask whether you have had a wide experience of women?'

'Some of my best friends are women,' I snapped, 'though I certainly wouidn't want my daughter to marry one of them.'

'I see. Well, I think we need not keep you from your journey any longer, Sir. The sheriff will be told that you did not kill Mr Krampf and since you no longer seem to be a possible embarrassment to Washington we have no further interest in you just now. If we turn out to be wrong we shall, uh, be able to find you, of course.'

'Of course,' I agreed.

As they crossed the room I rummaged desperately in my poor jumbled brain and picked out the big, knobbly question that hadn't been asked.

'Who did kill Krampf?' I asked.

They paused and looked back at me blankly.

'We don't have the faintest idea. We came down here to do it ourselves so it doesn't matter too much.'

It was a lovely exit line, you must admit.

'Could I have a drop more whisky, Mr Charlie?'

'Yes, of course, Jock, do; it'll bring the roses back into your cheeks.'

'Ta. Glug, suck. Aarhh. Well, that's all right then, isn't it, Mr Charlie?'

I rounded on him savagely.

'Of course it's not all right, you sodding idiot, those two goons have every intention of stamping on both of us as soon as we're well away from here. Look, you think those deputies out there are pigs? Well, they're bloody suffragettes beside those two mealy-mouthed murderers – these are genuine Presidential trouble-shooters and the trouble is us.'

'I don't get it. Why di'n't they shoot us then?'

'Oh Christ Jock, look, would Mr Martland shoot us if he thought it was a good idea?'

'Yeah, 'course.'

'But would he do it in Half Moon Street Police Station in front of all the regular coppers?'

'No, 'course not. Oh, I get it. Ooh.'

'I'm sorry I called you a sodding idiot, Jock.'

'That's all right, Mr Charlie, you was a bit worked up, I expect.'

'Yes, Jock.'

The sheriff came in and gave us back the contents of our pockets, including my Banker's Special. The cartridges were in a separate envelope. He was no longer urbane, he hated us now very much.

'I have been instructed,' he said, like a man spitting out fish-bones, 'not to book you for the murder you committed yesterday. There is a cab outside and I would like for you to get into it and get out of this county and never come back.' He shut his eyes very tightly and kept them shut as though hoping to wake up in a different time stream, one in which C. Mortdecai and J. Strapp had never been born.

We tiptoed out.

The deputies were in the outer office, standing tall, wearing the mindless sneers of their kind. I walked up close to the larger and nastier of the two.

'Your mother and father only met once,' I said carefully, 'and money changed hands. Probably a dime.'

As we pushed the street door open Jock said, 'What's a dime in English money, Mr Charlie?'

A huge, dishevelled car was quaking and farting at the curb outside. The driver, an evident alcoholic, told us that it was a fine evening and I could not find it in my heart to contradict him. He explained, as we climbed in, that he had another passenger to pick up en route and there she was on the next corner, as sweet and saucy a little wench as you could wish for.

She sat between us, smoothing her minimal print skirt over her naughty dimpled thighs and smiling up at us like a fallen angel. There's nothing like a pretty little girl to take a fellow's mind off his troubles, is there, especially when she looks as though she can be had. She told us that her name was Cinderella Gottschalk and we believed her – I mean, she couldn't have made it up, could she – and Jock gave her the last drink in the bottle. She said that she declared it was real crazy drinking liquor or words to that effect. She wore her cute little breasts high up under her chin, the way they used to in the 'fifties, *you* remember. In short, we had become firm friends and were ten miles out of town before a car behind us hit its siren and pulled out alongside. Our driver was giggling as he pulled over to the side and stopped. The official car shrieked to a rocking halt across our bows and out leaped the same two deputies, wearing the same sneers and pointing the same pistols.

'Oh my Gawd,' said Jock – a phrase I have repeatedly asked him not to use – 'what now?'

'They probably forgot to ask me where I get my hair done,' I said bravely. But it wasn't that. They yanked the door open and addressed our little Southern Belle.

'Parm me, Miss, how old are you?'

'Why, Jed Tuttle,' she sniggered, 'you know mah age jest as well as . . .'

'The age, Cindy,' he snapped.

'Rising fourteen,' she simpered, with a coy pout.

My heart sank.

'All right, you filthy deviates – out!' said the deputy.

They didn't hit us when they got us back to the office, they were going off duty and had no time to spare. They simply bunged us into the Tank.

'See you in the morning,' they told us, cosily.

'I demand to make a phone call.'

'In the morning, maybe, when you're sober.'

They left us there without even saying goodnight.

The Tank was a cube composed entirely of bars, except for the tiled floor which was covered with a thin crust of old vomit. The only furniture was an open plastic bucket which had not been emptied lately. Several kilowatts of fluorescent lighting poured pitilessly down from the ceiling high above. I could find no adequate words, but Jock rose to the occasion.

'Well, fuck this for a game of darts,' he said.

'Just so.'

We went to the corner furthest from the slop pail and propped our weary bodies against the bars. Much later, the night duty deputy appeared – an enormous, elderly fatty with a huge face like a bishop's bottom, rosy and round and hot. He stood by the Tank and sniffed with a pained expression on his nose.

'Youse stink like a coupla pigs or sompn,' he said, wagging his great head. 'Never could figure out how growed-up men could get theirselves in sich a state. I get drunk myself, times, but I don't get myself all shitten up like pigs or sompn.'

'It isn't us stinking,' I said politely, 'it's mostly this bucket. Do you think you could take it away?'

'Nope. We got a cleaning lady for them chores and she's to home by now. Anyways, say I take the bucket away, what you gonna spew into?'

'We don't *want* to be sick. We're not drunk. We're British diplomats and we protest strongly at this treatment, there's going to be a big scandal when we get out of here, why don't you let us make a phone call and do yourself a bit of good?'

He stroked his great face carefully, all over; it took quite a while.

'Nope,' he said at last. 'Have to ask the sheriff and he's to home by now. He don't admire to be disturbed at home 'cept for homicide of white Caucasians.'

'Well, at least give us something to sit on, couldn't you: I mean, *look* at the floor – and this suit cost me, ah, four hundred dollars.'

That fetched him, it was something he could understand. He came closer and studied my apparel carefully. Desperate for his sympathy, I straightened up and pirouetted, arms outstretched.

'Son,' he said finally, 'you was robbed. Why, you could buy that same suit in Albuquerque for a hunnerd-eighty-fi'.'

But he did pass a handful of newspapers through the bars to us before he left, shaking his head. He was one of Nature's gentlemen, I daresay.

We spread the papers on the least squamous section of the floor and lay down; the smell was not so bad at ground level. Sleep coshed me mercifully before I could even begin to dread the morrow.

16

My first thought was, he lied in every word.
Childe Roland

The sun rose like a great, boozy, red face staring into mine. On closer inspection it proved to be a great, boozy, red face staring into mine. It was also smiling stickily.

'Wake up, son,' the night deputy was saying, 'you got a visitor – and you got bail!'

I sprang to my feet and sat down again promptly, squealing at the pain in my kidneys. I let him help me up but Jock managed by himself – he wouldn't take the time of day from a policeman. Behind the deputy there gangled a long, sad man trying hard to smile out of a mouth designed only for refusing credit. He paid out a few yards of arm with a knobbly hand on the end of it which shook mine unconvincingly. For a moment I thought I recognized him.

'Krampf,' he said.

I studied the word but could make nothing of it as a conversational opening. In the end I said, 'Krampf?'

'Dr Milton Krampf III,' he agreed.

'Oh, sorry. C. Mortdecai.'

We let go of each other's hands but went on mumbling civilities. Meanwhile the night deputy lumbered round me, brushing off bits of nastiness from my suit.

'Piss off,' I hissed at him finally – a phrase well-adapted to hissing.

Jock and I needed to wash; Krampf said he would complete the formalities of bail and collect our belongings while we did so. In the washroom I asked Jock whether he had yet recovered the key to the suitcase.

'Christ, Mr Charlie, I only swallowed it dinnertime, di'n't I, and I haven't *been* since then.'

'No, that's right. I say, you couldn't sort of try now, could you?'

'No, I couldn't. I just been thinking about whether I could and I can't. I expect it's the change of water, always binds me.'

'Rubbish, Jock, you know you don't drink water. Did you have much chilli sauce with your hamburgers?'

'What, that hot stuff? Yeah.'

'Oh good.'

The night deputy was dancing about in agony of apology: it appeared that one of the deputies had taken my pistol with him, so as to drop it off at the forensic laboratory in the morning. This was bad news, for our only other weapon was Jock's Luger in the suitcase, whose key was, as it were, *in petto*. He offered to telephone for it but I had no wish to tarry: there was a teleprinter in the outer office and at any moment the British Embassy would be replying to the inquiries which someone must have put in train. The Ambassador had made it clear, you will recall, that the protection of the grand old British flag was not for me and, once repudiated, my diplomatic passport was about as valid as a nine-shilling note.

Outside, the night was as black as Newgate's knocker and the rain was crashing down; when it rains in those parts it really puts its heart into the job. We dived into Krampf's big pale car – with a nice social sense he shunted Jock into the back seat with suitcase. I asked him civilly where he was thinking of taking us.

'Why, I thought you might care to come visit with me a little,' he said easily. 'We have this kind of very private summer residence on the Gulf Coast – mine now, I guess – and that's where the pictures are. Especially the special ones, you know? You'll want to see them.'

'Oh Christ,' I thought, 'that's all I need. The mad millionaire's secret hideaway full of hot old masters and cool young mistresses.'

'That will be delightful,' I said. Then, 'May I ask you how you contrived to rescue us so opportunely, Dr Krampf?'

'Surely, it was easy. Yesterday I was a pretentious *kunstkenner* with a rich daddy – in my whole life I have earned maybe a hundred dollars by art history. Today I am a hundred million dollars – give or take a few million which Johanna gets – and that sort of money gets anybody out of jail here. I don't mean you bribe with it or anything like that, you just have to have it. Oh, I guess you mean how did I come to be *here?* That's easy, too; I flew in about noon to the ranch to arrange about shipping the body, it'll be on its way as soon as the police are finished with it. Family mausoleum is up in Vermont; good thing it's summer – in winter the ground gets so hard up there they just sharpen one end and hammer you into the ground, ha, ha.'

'Ha ha,' I agreed. I never liked my father, either, but I wouldn't have spoken of him as 'it' the day after his death.

'The police at the rancho heard about the Rolls and, uh, the other auto piling up and later they heard you'd been apprehended. Two guys from the FBI or some other Federal setup were there by then and they left soon after, said they were coming on here. I followed as soon as I'd sorted things out, in case they were being stupid. I mean, I knew that a man with your views on Giorgione couldn't be all bad, ha ha. Yeah, *sure* I know your work, I read *Burlington Magazine* every month, it's essential reading. I mean, for instance, you can't fully understand the achievement of Mondrian until you understand how Mantegna paved the way for him.'

I gagged quietly.

'Which reminds me,' he went on, 'I believe you were bringing my father a certain canvas; would you like to tell me where it is? I guess it's mine now?'

I said I guessed it was. The Spanish Government, of course, probably held a different view, but then they think they own Gibraltar too, don't they?

'It's in the Rolls, lined into the soft-top. I'm afraid you'll have a little difficulty retrieving it but at least it's safe for the time being, what? Oh, by the way, there's a little formality at the box office which your father didn't live to complete.'

'Oh?'

'Yes. Sort of, fifty thousand pounds, really.'

'Isn't that rather cheap, Mr Mortdecai?'

'Ah, well, you see the chap who actually swiped it has already been paid; the fifty thou is just my own little sort of *pourboire*.'

'I get it. Well, how and where do you want it? Swiss bank, numbered account, I guess?'

'Goodness, no, I should hate to think of it lying there in amongst all that chocolate and horrid Gruyère cheese and Alps. Do you think you could get it to Japan for me?'

'Surely. We have this development firm in Nagasaki; we'll retain you as, oh, aesthetic consultant on a five-year contract at, say, £11,000 a year. O.K.?'

'Six years at £10,000 would suit me just as well.'

'You have a deal.'

'Thank you very much.'

He shot me such an honest glance that I almost believed he meant it. He didn't, naturally. I don't mean that he begrudged me the fifty thousand – he hadn't been rich long enough to start being stingy about money. No, what I mean is that, quite clearly, I was now surplus to his requirements in all sorts of ways and allowing me to live much longer could form no part of his programme. Having sound views on Giorgione didn't carry with it the privilege of staying alive; why, I might linger on for years, a misery to myself and a burden to others.

We chatted on.

He didn't seem to know much about the relining process – surprising, really, in an authority on the Moderns, when you consider that the average modern picture is in need of attention within five years of the paint drying; indeed, many of them are cracking or flaking off the canvas long before that.

It's not that they couldn't learn proper techniques if they wanted to; I think it's because they're sort of subconsciously *shy* about posterity seeing their work.

'Are you sure,' Krampf kept saying, 'that this, uh, process will not have damaged the picture?'

'Look,' I said at last, 'pictures aren't damaged that way. To damage a picture thoroughly you need a stupid housewife with a rag and some ammonia, or methylated spirits, or a good proprietary picture-cleaning fluid. You can slash a picture to ribbons and a good liner and restorer will have it back as good as new before you can cough – remember the Rokeby Venus?'

'Yes,' he said. 'Suffragette with an axe, wasn't it?'

'And you can paint another picture over it and the restorer – perhaps centuries later – will clean back to the original – no bother. Remember your father's Crivelli?'

His ears pricked up and the car wobbled.

'Crivelli? No. What Crivelli? Did he have a Crivelli? A good one?'

'It was a very good one, Bernardo Tatti said so. Your father bought it somewhere in the Veneto in 1949 or '50. You know how they sell Old Masters in Italy – the important ones hardly ever go through commercial galleries. As soon as someone with serious money makes it known that he's in the market for serious works of art he will find himself invited to a palazzo for the week-end. His titled host will very delicately indicate that he has to pay a lot of taxes in the near future – and *that's* a joke in Italy – and may be forced, even, to sell an Old Master or two.

'Your father bought the Crivelli like that. It bore certificates by the greatest experts: they always do, of course. *You* know. The subject was the Virgin and Child with a bare bottom and lots of pears and pomegranates and melons – quite lovely. Like the Frick Crivelli, but smaller.

'The Duke or Count hinted that he wasn't *quite* certain of his title to the picture but he could see that your father wasn't a man to fuss about such trifles – it had to be smuggled out in any case, because of the law against export of works of art. Your father took it to an artist friend in Rome who gave it a coat of size then daubed a piece of Futurist-Vorticist rubbish on top. (Sorry, forgot that was your field.) Boldly signed and dated 1949, it went through the customs with no more than a pitying glance.

'Back in the States, he sent it to the best restorer in New York with a note saying, "Clean off modern overpaint; restore and expose original." After a few weeks he sent the restorer one of his cables – you know – "REPORT IMMEDIATELY PROGRESS ON QUOTE MODERN UNQUOTE PAINTING."

'The restorer cabled back, "HAVE REMOVED QUOTE MOD-ERN UNQUOTE PAINTING STOP HAVE REMOVED QUOTE CRIVELLI UNQUOTE MADONNA STOP AM DOWN TO POR-TRAIT OF MUSSOLINI STOP WHERE DO I STOP QUERY."'

Dr Krampf didn't laugh. He looked straight ahead, his knuckles tight on the wheel. After a while I said diffidently, 'Well, your father came to think it very funny indeed after the first shock. And your father was not easily amused.'

'My father was a simple-minded, sex-crazed jerk,' he said evenly. 'What had he given for the picture?' I told him and he winced. Conversation flagged. The car went a little faster.

After a while Jock cleared his throat sheepishly.

'Excuse me, Mr Charlie, could you ask Dr Crump to stop some-where soon? I got to go to the bog. Call of nature,' he added, by way of a grace note.

'Really, Jock,' I said sternly, to conceal my pleasure, 'you should have thought of that before you came out. It's all that chilli sauce, I expect.

We stopped at an all-night diner attached to a motel. Twenty minutes later, crammed with distressful fried eggs, we decided that we might as well spend what was left of the night there. Jock passed me the suitcase key, as good as new: I had expected to see it pitted and corroded by his powerful digestive juices.

I locked my door although I was pretty sure Krampf would bide his time until he had us in his kind-of-very-private summer residence. As I climbed into bed I decided that I must make a careful, objective analysis of my situation in the light of facts alone. 'If hopes were dupes,' I told myself, 'fears may be liars.' Surely the razor-keen Mortdecai brain could think its way out of this nasty, but after all primitive, mess.

Unfortunately the razor-keen brain fell asleep as soon as its con-tainer hit the pillow. *Most* unfortunately, really, as it turned out.

17

And, thus we half-men struggle. At the end,
God, I conclude, compensates, punishes.
Andrea del Sarto

How sharper than a serpent's tooth is an awakening without tea! Jock, honest fellow, brought me all sorts of motel provender but tea was not amongst those present. If Paris, as Galiani says, is the café of Europe, then the US of A must be the hot-dog stand of the world. 'Faugh!' I said, but I ate some to please Jock.

It was nearly noon; I had slept a solid eight hours. Bathed, shaved and dressed in my nattiest, I sallied out into the morning sunshine, full of the spirit of Sir Percy Blakeney-Mortdecai, *le Bouton Ecarlate*. '*A la lanterne* with Citoyen de Krampf', I murmured, flicking a speck of snot from the irreproachable Méchlin lace of my jabot.

There was a powder-blue Buick outside.

A.L. Rowse once said that making a really important historical discovery is very like sitting, inadvertently, on a cat. I felt, at that moment, like just such an historian – and, indeed, like just such a cat. Dr Krampf, who was in the driving seat, cannot have failed to notice my standing high jump and my strangled squeal, but he elaborately gave no sign of surprise. Jock and I got in, for it was evidently the car we had arrived in, and after a certain amount of good-morning swapping we set off.

This way and that, like Odysseus on so many occasions, I divided my swift mind. The suitcase key, the fruit of Jock's honest labours, was twice blessed: it had furnished me with clean underwear and Jock with his friendly neighbourhood Luger – a pretty strong partnership.

My diplomatic passport would probably pass muster in most smaller airports for perhaps another twenty-four hours, though hardly longer. We were two, Krampf at present but one. I was pretty certain that he was thinking of abolishing me – owners of powder-blue Buicks could be no friends of mine and I knew far too much about the provenance of his newly inherited collection and little things like who-killed-daddy – but he cannot have known for certain that we knew this. He, it was clear, had to get us to ground of his own choosing before he could fit us for cement overcoats – if that's the phrase I want – but we were now in a position to dissuade him.

We drove on, south and east, stopping for a horrid lunch at a place called Fort Stockton, where I surreptitiously bought a map and studied it, locked in the used-beer department. Then we drove some more, across the Pecos river toward Sonora. (Just place names now, all magic gone.) Just before Sonora I said to Krampf, 'I'm sorry, my dear chap, but we can't after all stay with you this weekend.' He kept his hands on the wheel but boggled at me sideways.

'How d'you mean?'

'Something came up, you see.'

'I don't get it – what could have come up?'

'Well, as a matter of fact, I've just received a cable.'

'You've just receive a c . . .?'

'Yes, reminding me of a subsequent engagement. So perhaps you'd be awfully kind and turn north at Sonora?'

'Mr Mortdecai, I know this is some kind of a joke so I'm just going to keep right on for the Gulf, heh heh. Mind you,' he chuckled, 'if I didn't know your pistol was back in the forensic laboratory I'd be tempted to take you seriously, heh heh.'

'Jock, show Dr Krampf the Luger.' Jock showed him, leaning over from the back seat. Krampf looked at it carefully; he saw, if he knew about Lugers, the little *Geladen* indicator sticking up above the breech; then he accelerated, a sensible thing to do, for no one gives the *gesnickschuss* to a chap driving at seventy m.p.h.

'Jock, the point of the left shoulder, please.' Jock's great fist, brass-shod, came down like a steam hammer and I steadied the wheel as Krampf's arm went dead.

He slowed down and stopped: you can't drive properly when you're crying. I changed places with him rapidly and we continued – I had a feeling you're not allowed to loiter on Interstate Highway 10. He just sat there beside me nursing his arm, saying nothing, looking straight ahead through his tears. A sure confirmation of naughty intent, for an honest man would be protesting volubly, wouldn't he?

Abilene is a hundred and fifty miles north of Sonora; we did a lot of those miles in the next two hours and Krampf still just sat there, apparently unafraid; his faith in the power of a hundred million dollars still unshaken. After San Angelo – I sang 'E lucevan le stelle' as we passed through: opera lovers will know why – I started looking about for likely spots, for the evenings were drawing in, and soon after crossing the Colorado I found one, an unnumbered dirt road which followed the bed of a dry river. Satisfied that we could not be overlooked, I got out, urging Krampf before me.

'Krampf,' I said, 'I fear you wish me ill. At present it is no part of my plans to have Krampfs after my blood as well as everyone else, so I must thwart your designs on my person. Do I make myself clear? I propose to leave you here, securely bound, warmly clad but without any money. At the airport I shall write to the police telling them where to look for you and enclosing your money, for I am not that kind of a thief. You are unlikely to die before they find you. Any questions?'

He looked at me levelly, wondering whether he could get my liver out with his fingernails. He didn't say anything, nor did he spit.

'Wallet,' I said, snapping my fingers. He brought out a slim snakeskin job and tossed it rudely at my feet. I picked it up, I'm not proud. It contained a driving licence, several of the better sort of credit cards, photographs of some hideous children and a portrait of Madison. The portrait, of course, was on a thousand dollar bill.

'No small money?' I asked. 'No, I suppose not. You wouldn't like handling it, you'd know where it had been. And you don't look like a heavy tipper.'

'Mr Charlie,' said Jock, 'rich blokes over here don't keep ordinary money in their wallets, they have it in their trousers in a sort of clip made out of a gold coin.'

'You're right, Jock, full marks. Krampf, the bill-clip, please.'

He reached grudgingly for his hip pocket, too grudgingly, and suddenly I realized what else was there: I aimed a swift kick at his goolies, he stepped back, stumbled and dragged out the Lilliput pistol as he fell. I didn't hear the shot but my left arm seemed to be torn out by the roots and as I fell I saw Jock's boot connecting with Krampf's head.

I must have faded out for a few moments; the pain was excruciating. When I came to, Jock was dabbing at my armpit with a dressing from the car's first-aid kit; the little bullet had passed along my armpit, shredding it horridly but missing the axillary artery by enough millimetres for safety. It was a very good first-aid box: when we had stanched the bleeding and done an adequate bandage job we turned our attention to the motionless Krampf.

'Tie him up now, Jock, while he's still out.'

A long pause.

'Uh, Mr Charlie, uh, would you have a look at him?'

I looked. The side of his head felt like a bag of Smith's Potato Crisps. Another generation of Krampfs had carried its bat to the Eternal Pavilion to have a word with the Great Scorer.

'Really, Jock, you are too bad,' I snapped. 'That's twice in two days. If I've told you once I've told you a dozen times, I *will* not have you killing chaps all the time.'

'Sorry, Mr Charlie,' he said sulkily. 'But I di'n't mean to, did I? I mean, I was saving your life, wasn't I?'

'Yes, Jock, I suppose you were. I'm sorry if I spoke hastily – I am in some pain, you realize.'

We buried him darkly at dead of night, the sods with our bayonets turning, as you might say. Then we listened for a long time, drove quietly back to the main road and on to Abilene.

There were planes from Abilene that night to Denver and to Kansas City; Jock and I took one each.

'See you in Quebec, then, Jock,' I said.

'O.K., Mr Charlie.'

18

The Bactrian was but a wild, childish man,
And could not write nor speak, but only loved:
So, lest the memory of this go quite,
Seeing that I to-morrow fight the beasts,
I tell the same to Pboebas, whom believe!

A Death in the Desert

You must have noticed that until now my tangled tale has observed at least some of the unities proper to tragedy: I have not tried to relate what other people thought or did when this was outside my knowledge; I have not whisked you hither and yon without suitable transport and I have never started a sentence with the words 'some days later'. Each morning has witnessed the little death of a heavy drinker's awakening and 'each slow dusk a drawing down of blind'. The English, as Raymond Chandler has pointed out, may not always be the best writers in the world but they are incomparably the best dull writers.

If I have not always made clear the *rationale* of these events, it is partly because you are probably better at that sort of thing than I am and partly because I confess myself quite bemused by finding that the events which I thought I was controlling were in fact controlling me.

It has amused me, these last few weeks, to cast my recollections into some sort of disciplined mould but this foolishness must now cease, for the days are drawing in and time's helicopter beats the air furiously over my head. Events have overtaken literature: there is time for a few more leisured pages and then perhaps for some journal jottings; after that, I suspect, no time at all, ever.

It looks as though, by a piece of vulgar irony, I have come home to die within sight of the scenes of my hated childhood: the ways of Providence are indeed unscrupulous, as Pat once said to Mike as they were walking down Broadway – or was it O'Connell Street?

Getting here was easy. We flew from Quebec to Eire in the same aircraft but not together. At Shannon, Jock walked straight through Immigration waving his Tourist Passport, they didn't even look at it. He was carrying the suitcase. He took a domestic flight to Collinstown Airport, Dublin, and waited for me at a nice pub called Jury's in College Green.

For my part, I spent a quiet hour in the lavatory at Shannon with half a bottle of whisky, mingled with various groups of travellers, told all and sundry that my wife, children and luggage were in planes headed for Dublin, Belfast and Cork, and wept myself tiresomely and bibulously out and into a taxi without anyone asking for a passport. I think perhaps they were rather glad to get rid of me. The taxi driver milked me systematically of currency all the way to Mullingar, where I shaved, changed clothes and accent, and took another taxi to Dublin.

Jock was at Jury's as arranged, but only barely; in another few minutes he would have been ejected for he was pissed as a pudding and someone had taught him a naughty phrase in Erse which he kept singing to the tune of 'The Wearing of the Boyne' or whatever they call it.

We took a cheap night flight to Blackpool, and only acted drunk enough to fit in with the rest of the passengers. The airport staff were waiting to go to bed or wherever people go in Blackpool: they turned their backs on the whole lot of us. We took separate taxis to separate small and hateful hotels. I had potato pie for supper, I don't know what Jock had.

In the morning we took separate trains and met, by arrangement, in the buffet on Carnforth Station. You may never have heard of Carnforth but you must have seen the station, especially the buffet, for it was there that they made *Brief Encounter* and it is sacred to the memory of Celia Johnson. Nowadays Carnforth has no other claim to fame: once a thriving steel town with an important railway junction, today it is distinguished only by the singular, and clearly *intentional,* ugliness of every building and by the extraordinary niceness of the people who inhabit them – even the bank managers. I was born five miles away, at a place called Silverdale.

Carnforth is in the extreme northwest corner of Lancashire and has sometimes called itself the Gateway to the Lake District. It is not quite on the coast, it is not quite anything, really. There are some good pubs. There used to be a cinema when I was a boy but I was never allowed to go, and it's closed now. Except for Bingo, naturally.

One of the hotels is kept by a nice fat old Italian called Dino something; he's known me since I was a *bambino*. I told him that I was just back from America where I had made some enemies and that I had to lie low.

'Donter worry Mr Charlie, thoser bloddy Sicilian bosstuds donter find you here. If I see them hang around I get the police bloddy quick – are good boys here, not afraid ofer stinking Mafiosi.'

'It's not really quite like that, Dino. I think if you see anyone you'd better just let me know quietly.'

'O.K., Mr Charlie.'

'Thank you, Dino. *Evviva Napoli!*

'*Abassa Milano!*'

'*Cazzone pendente!*' we cried in chorus – our old slogan from years ago.

Jock and I stayed there in close retirement for perhaps five weeks until my armpit was healed and I had grown a more or less plausible beard. (I want to make it quite clear that Dino had no idea that we had done anything wrong.) I stopped dyeing my hair and eating starchy foods and soon I looked a well-preserved seventy. Finally, before venturing out, I removed both my upper canine teeth, which are attached to a wire clip: with my upper incisors resting lightly on the lower lip I look the picture of senile idiocy, it always makes Mrs Spon *shriek*. I let my now grizzled hair grow long and fluffy, bought a pair of good field-glasses and mingled with the bird watchers. It's astonishing how many there are nowadays: ornithology used to be an arcane hobby for embittered schoolmasters, dotty spinsters and lonely little boys but now it is as normal a weekend occupation as rug-making or wife-swapping. I was terribly keen on it when I was at school, so I knew the right cries and, as a matter of fact, I became rather keen again and thoroughly enjoyed my outings.

This part of Lancashire contains some of the best bird-watching terrain in England: sea and shore birds in their millions haunt the vast salt-marshes and tidal flats of Morecambe Bay, and the reeds of Leighton Moss – an RSPB sanctuary – are alive with duck, swans, gulls and even the bittern.

I gave Dino three hundred pounds and he bought me a second-hand dark-green Mini, registered in his name. I plastered on a few stickers – SAVE LEVENS HALL, VOTE CONSERVATIVE, VISIT STEAM-TOWN – and dumped a Karri-Kot in the back seat: an inspired piece of camouflage, you must admit. We contrived to get a pair of tinted contact lenses for Jock, changing his startling blue eyes to a dirty brown. He liked them very much, called them 'me shades'.

Meanwhile, since Carnforth is on STD now, it was safe to dial a number of guarded calls to London, where various naughty friends, in exchange for a lot of money, set to work creating new identities for Jock and me, so that we could get to Australia and start a new life amongst the Sheilas and Cobbers. New identities are very expensive and take a long time, but the process of obtaining them is so much easier now that there are all these drugs about. You simply find a chap who's on the big H-for-heroin and not long for this world, preferably a chap with at least some points of resemblance to you. You take him under your wing – or rather your naughty friends do – lodge him, supply him with H and feed him whenever he can gag anything down. You get his National Insurance Card paid up to date, buy him a passport, open a Post Office Savings Account in his name, pass the driving test for him and fix him up with an imaginary job at a real place. (The 'employer' gets his wages back in cash, doubled.) Then you pay a very expensive craftsman to substitute your photograph in the new passport and you're a new man.

(The drug addict, of course, now becomes a bit superfluous: you can have him knocked off professionally but that's an extra, and awfully expensive nowadays. The best and cheapest course is to deprive him of his medicine for three days or so until he's quite beside himself, then leave him in a busy public lavatory – Piccadilly Under-

ground is much favoured in the trade – with a syringe containing a
heavy overdose, and let Nature take its kindly course. The coroner
will scarcely glance at him: he's probably better off where he is; why,
he might have lingered on for years, etc.)

In short, all seemed well except that William Hickey or one of
those columnists had once or twice dropped delicate hints that certain
People in High Places had been receiving certain photographs, which
might or might not have referred to the Hockbottle art work. If so, I
couldn't really see who could be doing it – surely not Johanna? One
of Hockbottle's horrid friends? *Martland?* I didn't let it worry me.

Last night, when I walked into the bar of Dino's hotel, full of
fresh air and nursing a splendid appetite, I would have told anyone
that things were going uncommonly well. I had spent the afternoon
on the Moss and had been fortunate enough to have had a pair of
Bearded Tits in my field-glasses for several minutes – and if you
think there's no such bird you can jolly well look it up in the nearest
bird book. That was last night, only.

Last night when I walked into the bar

The barman should have smiled and said, 'Evening, Mr Jackson, what
do you fancy?' I mean, that's what he'd said to me every evening for
weeks.

Instead he gave me a hostile stare and said, 'Well, Paddy, usual I
suppose?' I was completely taken aback.

'Come on,' said the barman disagreeably, 'make your mind up.
There's other people want serving, you know.'

Two strangers at the end of the bar studied me casually in the
mirror behind the display bottle. I twigged.

'Arl roight arl roight,' I growled thickly, 'av coorse Oi'll have me
usual, ye cross-grained little sod.'

He pushed a double Jameson's Irish whisky across the bar at me.

'And watch your language,' he said, 'or you can get out.'

'Bollocks,' I said and tossed the whisky back messily. I wiped
my mouth with the back of my hand, belched and lurched out. It is a
good thing that a serious ornithologist's field clothes are more or less

the same as an Irish navvy's drinking kit. I fled upstairs and found Jock sitting on the bed, reading the *Beano*.

'Come on,' I said, 'they're on to us.'

We had kept in a state of readiness for any emergency so we were out of the hotel by the kitchen entrance some ninety seconds after I had left the bar, heading for the station yard where I had parked the Mini. I started the engine and backed out of the slot; I was quite calm, there was no reason for them to have suspected me.

Then I cursed, stalling the engine, paralysed with dismay.

'Smatter, Mr Charlie, forgotten something?'

'No, Jock. Remembered something.'

I had remembered that I had not paid for my whisky – and that the barman had not asked me to do so. Drunken Irish navvies hardly ever have charge accounts at respectable provincial hotels.

I got the engine started again, jammed the gears cruelly into mesh and swung out of the yard into the street. A man standing at the corner turned and raced beck towards the hotel. I prayed that their car was pointing in the wrong direction.

I rammed the unprotesting little Mini out of town to the north on the Millhead Road; just before the second railway bridge I doused the lights and whisked it off to the left, towards Hagg House and the marsh. The road dwindled to a footpath and then to a wet track; we squashed barbed wire, nosed our way down banks, half-lifted the Mini across the impossibly soft parts, cursed and prayed and listened for the sounds of pursuit. To our left some three-headed spawn of Cerberus started to yelp and yap dementedly. We continued west, hating the dog with a deep, rich hatred, and found the River Keer by pitching into it. To be exact, the Mini had pitched down its bank and come to rest, nose downward, in the squishy sand beside the channel, for the tide was far out. I grabbed the almost empty suitcase, Jock grabbed the knapsack and we scrambled into the stream, gasping with shock as the cold water reached groin level. At the far side we stopped before scaling the bank and showing ourselves on the skyline; half a mile behind us an engine raced in a low gear; two cones of light from headlamps waved about in the sky, then suddenly went out.

The stars were bright but we were too far away to be seen by our pursuers; we scrambled up the bank – how I blessed my new-found physical fitness – and made off northwestwards, heading towards the lights of Grange-Over-Sands, six miles away across the glistening mud flats.

It was quite unlike anything that has ever happened to me, it was the strangest journey I have ever made. The darkness, the unheard, nearby sea, the whistle and bleat of the wings of flocks of bewildered birds, the slap of our feet on the wet sand and the *fear* that drove us on towards the wriggling lights so far across the bay.

But I had this much going for me: I was on familiar ground. My plan was to strike Quicksand Pool – a two-mile treacherous lagoon – at its most dangerous point, then turn northeastwards and follow it to its narrowest part and cross there. At that point, the friendly shore of Silverdale would bear due north at two miles' distance. This depended on our having crossed the Keer at the right spot, and on the tide being where I believed it to be – I had no choice but to assume that I was right about both.

That was where the nightmare began.

Jock was loping a few yards to my left when we both found ourselves on quaking ground. I did what you should do in such a case – keep moving fast but circle back sharply to your starting point. Jock didn't. He stopped, grunted, tried to pull back, splashed about, stuck fast. I dropped the suitcase and hunted for him in the dark while he called to me, his voice high with panic as I had never heard it before. I got hold of his hand and started to sink also; I threw myself down, only my elbows now on the quagmire. It was like pulling at an oak tree. I knelt to get better purchase but my knees sank straight in, terrifyingly.

'Lie forward,' I snarled at him.

'Can't, Mr Charlie – I'm up to me belly.'

'Wait, I'll get the suitcase.'

I had to strike a match to find the suitcase, then another to find Jock again in the tantalizing shimmer of wet sand and starshine. I thrust the suitcase forward and he laid his arms on it, hugging it to his chest, driving it into the mud as he bore down on it.

'No good, Mr Charlie,' he said at last. I'm up to me armpits and I can't breathe much any more.' His voice was a horrid travesty.

Behind us – not nearly far enough behind us – I heard the rhythmic patter of feet on wet sand.

'Go on, Mr Charlie, scarper!'

'Christ, Jock, what do you think I am?'

'Don't be stupid,' he gasped. 'Piss off. But do me a favour first. You know. I don't want it like this. Might take half an hour. Go on, *do* it.'

'Christ, Jock,' I said again, appalled.

'Go on, me old mate. Quick. Put the leather in.'

I scrambled to my feet, aghast. Then I couldn't bear the noises he was making any more and I stepped on to the suitcase with my left foot and trod on his head with my right foot, grinding at it. He made dreadful noises but his head wouldn't go under. I kicked at it frantically again and again, until the noises stopped, then I clawed up the suitcase and ran blindly, weeping with horror and terror and love.

When I heard the water chuckling below me I guessed my position and threw myself at the channel, not caring whether it was the crossing place or not. I got over, leaving my right shoe in the mud – *that* shoe, thank God – and ran north, each breath tearing at my windpipe. Once I fell and couldn't get up; behind me and to the left I saw torches flickering: perhaps one of them had gone to join Jock – I don't know, it's not important. I kicked the other shoe off and got up and ran again, cursing and weeping, falling into gullies, tearing my feet on stones and shells, the suitcase battering at my knees, until at last I crashed into the remains of the breakwater at Jenny Brown's Point.

There I pulled myself together a little, sitting on the suitcase, trying to think calmly, starting to learn to live with what had happened. No, with what I had done. With what I *have* done. A soft rain began to fall and I turned my face up to it, letting it rinse away some of the heat and the evil.

The knapsack was back at Quicksand Pool; all the necessities of life were in it. The suitcase was almost empty except for some packets of currency. I needed a weapon, shoes, dry clothes, food, a drink, shelter and – above all – a friendly word from someone, anyone.

Keeping the low limestone cliffs on my right hand I stumbled along the shore for almost a mile to Know End Point, where the salt-marsh proper begins – that strange landscape of sea-washed turf and gutters and flashes where the finest lambs in England graze.

Above me and to my right shone the lights of the honest bungalow dwellers of Silverdale: 1 found myself envying them bitterly. It is chaps like them who have the secret of happiness, they know the art of it, they always knew it. Happiness is an annuity, or it's shares in a Building Society; it's a pension and blue hydrangeas, and wonderfully clever grandchildren, and being on the Committee, and just-a-few-earlies in the vegetable garden, and being alive and wonderful-for-his-age when old so-and-so is under the sod, and it's doubleglazing and sitting by the electric fire remembering that time when you told the Area Manager where he got off and that other time when that Doris . . .

Happiness is easy: I don't know why more people don't go in for it.

I stole along the road leading up from the shore. My watch said 11.40. It was Friday, so licensing hours would have ended at eleven, plus ten minutes drinking-up time plus, say, another ten minutes getting rid of the nuisances. My soaked and ragged socks made wet whispers on the pavement. There were no cars outside the hotel, no lights on in front. I was starting to shake with cold and reaction and the hope of succour as I hobbled through the darkened car park and round to the kitchen window.

I could see the landlord, or joint proprietor as he prefers to be called, standing quite near the kitchen door; he was wearing the disgraceful old hat which he always puts on for cellar work and his face, as ever, was that of a hanging judge. He has watched my career with a jaundiced eye for some five and twenty years, on and off, and he has not been impressed.

He opened the kitchen door and looked me up and down impassively.

'Good evening, Mr Mortdecai,' he said, 'you've lost a bit of weight.'

'Harry,' I gabbled, 'you've got to help me. Please.'

'Mr Mortdecai, the last time you asked me for drinks after hours was in nineteen hundred and fifty-six. The answer is still no.'

'No, Harry, really. I'm in serious trouble.'

'That's right, Sir.'

'Eh?'

'I said – "that's right, Sir."'

'How d'you mean?'

'I mean two gentlemen were here inquiring after your where-abouts last evening, stating that they were from the Special Branch. They were most affable but they displayed great reluctance to produce their credentials when requested to do so.' He always talks like that.

I didn't say anything more, I just looked at him beseechingly. He didn't actually smile but his glare softened a little, perhaps.

'You'd better be off now, Mr Mortdecai, or you'll be disturbing my routine and I'll be forgetting to bolt the garden door or some-thing.'

'Yes. Well, thanks, Harry. Goodnight.'

'Goodnight, Charlie.'

I slunk back into the shadow of the squash court and crouched there in the rain with my thoughts. He had called me *Charlie,* he never had before. That was one for the book: that was the friendly word. Jock, at the end, had called me his old mate.

One by one the lights in the hotel went out. The church clock had struck half-past midnight with the familiar flatness before I crept round the building, through the rock terrace, and tied the garden door. Sure enough, someone had carelessly forgotten to bolt it. It gives on to a little sun-parlour with two sun-faded settees. I peeled off my drenched clothes, draped them on one settee and my wracked body on the other, with a grunt. As my eyes grew used to the dimness I dis-cerned a group of objects on the table between the settees. Someone had carelessly left a warm old topcoat there, and some woollen underclothes and a towel: also a loaf of bread, three quarters of a cold chicken, forty Embassy tipped cigarettes, a bottle of Teacher's whisky and a pair of tennis shoes. It's astonishing how careless some of these hoteliers are, no wonder they're always complaining.

It must have been four o'clock in the morning when I let myself out of the little sun-parlour. The moon had risen and luminous clouds were scudding across it at a great pace. I skirted the hotel and found the footpath behind it which goes across the Lots, those strangely contoured limestone downs clad with springy turf. I gave the Burrows' heifers the surprise of their lives as I jogged between them in the dark. It is only a few hundred yards to the Cove, where once the sailing ships from Furness unloaded ore for the furnace at Leighton Beck. Now, since the channels shifted, it is close-nibbled turf, covered with a few inches of sea-water two or three times a month.

What is more to the point, there is a cave in the cliff, below the inexplicable ivy-gnawed battlements which surmount it. It is an uninviting cave, even the children do not care to explore it, and there is reputed to be a sudden drop at the end of it, to an unplumbed pit. Dawn was making its first faint innuendos in the East as I clambered in.

I slept until noon out of sheer exhaustion, then ate some more of the bread and chicken and drank more of the Scotch. Then I went to sleep again: dreams would be bad, I knew, but waking thoughts for once were worse. I awoke in the late afternoon.

The light is fading rapidly now. Later tonight I shall call on my brother.

To be exact, it was in the early hours of this Sunday morning that I stole out of the cave and drifted up into the village through the dark. The last television set had been reluctantly switched off, the last poodle had been out for its last piddle, the last cup of Bournvita had been brewed. Cove Road was like a well-kept grave: husbands and wives lay dreaming of past excesses and future coffee-mornings, they gave out no vibrations, it was hard to believe they were there. A motor car approached, driven with the careful sedateness of a consciously drunk driver; I stepped into the shadows until it had passed. A cat rubbed itself against my right foot; a few days ago I would have kicked it without compunction but now I could not even kick my own brother. Not with that foot.

The cat followed me up the slope of Walling's Lane, mewing inquisitively, but it turned tail at the sight of the big white tom who crouched under the hedge like a phantom Dick Turpin. Lights were burning up at Yewbarrow and a strain of New Orleans jazz filtered down through the trees – old Bon would be settling down to an all-night poker and whisky session. As I turned right at Silver Ridge there was one brief deep bay from the St. Bernard, then no more sounds save for the whisper of my own feet along Elmslack. Someone had been burning garden rubbish and a ghost of the smell lingered – one of the most poignant scents in the world, at once wild and homely.

Off the lane I picked my way along the just discernible footpath which drops down to the back wall of Woodfields Hall, the seat of Robin, Second Baron Mortdecai, etc. Golly, what a name. He was born shortly before the Great War, as you can tell: it was *de rigueur* to call your son Robin in that decade and my mother was remorselessly *de rigueur,* as anyone could tell you, if nothing else.

You'd never guess where I am writing this. I'm sitting, knees doubled up to my chin, on my childhood's lavatory in the nursery wing of my brother's house. It has happier memories for me than most of the rest of the house, which is haunted by my father's cupidity and chronic envy, my mother's febrile regret at having married an impossible cad and now by my brother's crawling disgust at everything and everyone. Including himself. And especially me – he wouldn't spit in my face if it were on fire, unless he could spit petrol.

Beside me on the wall there is a roll of soft, pink lavatory paper: our nurse would never have allowed that, she believed in Spartan bums for the children of the upper classes and we had to use the old-fashioned, crackling, broken-glass variety.

I have just been in my old bedroom which is always kept ready for me, never altered or disturbed; just the kind of false note my brother loves sardonically to strike. He often says, 'Do remember that you always have a home here, Charlie,' then waits for me to look sick. Under a floorboard in my room I groped for and found a large oilskin package containing my first and favourite handgun, a 1920 Police and Military Model Smith and Wesson .455, the most beautiful heavy revolver ever designed. A few years ago, before I took up whisky as an indoor sport, I could do impressive things to a playing card with this pistol at twenty paces, and I am confident that I could still hit a larger target in a good light. Like, say, Martland.

There is one box of military ammunition for it – nickel jacketed and very noisy – and most of a box of plain lead target stuff, hand-loaded with a low powder charge, much more useful for what I have in mind. You wouldn't be allowed to use it in war, of course, that soft lead ball can do dreadful things to anything it hits, I'm happy to say.

I shall finish my bottle of Teacher's, with a wary eye on the door lest a long-dead Nanny should catch me, then go downstairs and visit my brother. I shall not tell him how I got into the house. I shall just let him worry about it, it's the sort of thing he does worry about. I have no intention of shooting him, it would be an inexcusable self-indulgence at this time. In any case, it would probably be doing him a favour and I owe him a lot of things but no favours.

I called him brother, Englishman and friend!

As I let myself quietly into the library, my brother Robin was sitting with his back to me, writing his memoirs with a scratchy noise. Without turning round or ceasing to scratch at the paper he said,

'Hullo, Charlie, I didn't hear anyone let you in?'

'Expecting me, Robin?'

'Everyone else knocks.' Pause. 'Didn't you have any trouble with the dogs as you came through the kitchen garden?'

'Look, those dogs of yours are as much use as tits on a warthog. If I'd been a burglar they'd have offered to hold my torch.'

'You'll be wanting a drink,' he said, flatly, insultingly.

'I've given it up, thanks.'

He stopped scribbling and turned round. Looked me up and down, slowly, caressingly.

'Going ratting?' he asked at last.

'No, you needn't worry tonight.'

'Would you like something to eat?'

'Yes, please. Not now,' I added as his hand went to the bell. 'I'll help myself later. Tell me who has been asking for me lately.'

'No village drabs with babies in their arms this year. Just a couple of comedians from some obscure branch of the Foreign Office, I didn't ask what they wanted. Oh, and a hard-faced bitch who said you'd been heard of in Silverdale and wanted to ask you to address the Lakeland Ladies' Etching Society or something of that sort.'

'I see. What did you tell them?'

'Said I thought you were in America, was that right?'

'Quite right, Robin. Thanks.' I didn't ask him how he knew I had been in America; he wouldn't have told me and I didn't really care. He sets aside a certain portion of his valuable time to following my doings, in the hopes that one day I'll give him an opening. He's like that.

'Robin, I'm on a Government assignment which I can't tell you about but it does involve getting quietly up into the Lake District and living rough for a few days – I need some stuff. A sleeping bag, some tinned food, a bicycle, torch, batteries, that sort of thing.' I watched him thinking how many of the items he could plausibly pretend not to have. I unbuttoned my coat, which fell open: the handle of the Smith and Wesson stuck up out of my waistband like a dog's leg.

'Come along,' he said cordially, 'let's see what we can rustle up.'

We rustled up everything in the end, although I had to remind him where some of the things were kept. I also took the Lake District sheet of the one-inch Ordnance Survey map to add colour to my fibs and two bottles of Black Label whisky.

'Thought you'd given it up, dear boy?'

'This is just for washing wounds out with,' I explained courteously.

I also took a bottle of turpentine. You, shrewd reader, will have guessed why, but he was mystified.

'Look,' I said as he let me out, 'please don't tell anyone, *anyone*, that I've been here, or where I'm going, will you?'

'Of course not,' he said warmly, looking me straight in the eye to show me his falseness. I waited.

'And Charlie . . .'

'Yes,' I said, face blank.

'Do remember, you always have a home here.'

'Thanks, old chap,' I replied gruffly.

As Hemingway says somewhere: even when you have learned not to answer letters, families have many ways of being dangerous.

Topheavy with my load of Boy-Scout dunnage, I pedalled errat-ically to the cemetery, then down Bottom's Lane, turned left at the Green and skirted Leighton Moss until I came to Crag Foot. I pushed the machine very quietly past the farm for fear of dogs and threaded my way up the broken road to the Crag.

The Crag is a sort of crag-shaped feature of limestone, rich in minerals and seamed with crevasses or 'grikes' as they call them here-abouts. It is a mile square on the map (SD 47:49,73) but it seems a great deal larger when you are trying to pick your way over it. Here, two hundred years ago, hoved the dreaded Three Fingered Jack, con-ning the Marsh with his spy-glass for unprotected travellers whose bones now lie full fathom five, enriching the greedy sands of Morecambe Bay. (Oh Jock – 'never shake thy gory locks at me!')

The Crag is riddled and pitted with holes of every sort, the Dog Hole, Fairy Hole, Badger Hole – all of which have given up ancient bones and implements – and forgotten shafts where minerals were dug in the vague past, and the foundations of immeasurably old stone huts and, highest of all, defence works made by the Ancient Britons themselves. It's a wonderful place for breaking a leg, even the poach-ers won't risk it at night. In front are the salt marshes and the sea, behind stands the Gothick beauty of Leighton Hall. To the right you can look down over the reedy haven of Leighton Moss and to your left there is the desolation of Carnforth.

Copper was the great thing to mine for here, long ago, but what I was aiming for was a certain paint mine. A red-oxide working, to be exact. Red-oxide or ruddle-mining was a thriving industry on the Crag once upon a time and the deserted shafts still weep a messy red-ness, the colour of a really vulgar Swiss sunset. It took me an hour to find the shaft I remembered best; it goes down steeply for ten feet, looking very wet and red, but then flattens out, turns right at an acute angle and becomes quite dry and airy. A friendly bramble now cloaks its entrance, I had the devil of a job fighting my way in.

19

So, I soberly laid my last plan
To extinguish the man.
Round his creep-hole, with never a break
Ran my fires for his sake;
Over-head, did my thunder combine
With my under-ground mine:
Till I looked from my labour content
To enjoy the event.

Instans Tyannus

Happiness is pear-shaped

'Playing it pear-shaped' was a favourite expression of Jock's; it seemed to mean deftly turning a situation to one's own advantage; seizing a favorable opportunity: Boxing Clever.

So the new, resourceful, *pear-shaped* Mortdecai arose at noon and brewed his own tea today over a little butane camping stove. Quite successfully. How about that, Kit Carson? Move over, Jim Bridger!

As I sipped it I tried to think the situation over carefully, examining it for neglected apertures, but to little avail – noon on Sunday has a special significance for some of us, you know; it is the time when the pubs open. The thought of all those happy drinkers bellying up to the bar counters in Silverdale and Warton kept driving all pear-shaped considerations out of my head. True, there was whisky, but noon on the Sabbath is sacred to bottled beer. I *wanted* some.

There hasn't been a soul on the Crag all day; I can't understand how people can frowst in public houses drinking bottled beer when there's all this splendid fresh air and scenery to be had for nothing. Even the campers, whose lurid tents and tasteful pastel caravans pimple the landscape here and there like dragon's teeth, are not in evidence: they're probably leading the simple life in front of their portable tellies, watching a nature programme, bless them. Most of them will be back in Bradford tomorrow, glowing with virtue and comparing mosquito bites.

I have taken the bicycle to pieces and wangled it all down into the cave. I've also been down to the icy spring which runs in a miniature canyon between two huge slabs of limestone; I washed myself all over, squeaking with the cold, and even drank a little of the water. It was delicious but I had to drink some Black Label when I got back up here, to take the taste away. It would never do to take up hydropathy at my age. Hydrophobia, yes, perhaps.

There is a most inaccessible spot above the mine where no one can creep up on you and I have built a small, discreet camp fire on which a can of baked beans is warming. From where I sit I can see the long necklace of Morecambe's lights – 'the bright boroughs, the circle-citadels there'.

Later

I like the 'wet and wilderness, weeds' of this place very much. It is quiet and no one has been near. I have been sleeping very happily, dreaming innocent dreams, listening to the sweet wild call of the redshanks whenever I wake. Now more than ever seems it sweet to die; the grave cannot be darker nor more solitary than this: nor stiller except when the wind, stirring the brambles at the entrance furtively, tries to frighten me. I recall the only really poignant ghost story

> *(Sexton:* 'What are you a-sniggering at?'
> *Ghost:* 'It's not funny enough for two.')

Another day – I'm not sure which, now

I saw a marsh-harrier this morning; it quartered the reed beds of the Moss for a time, then flew strongly across Slackwood Farm to vanish in Fleagarth Wood. There's a new tent in Fleagarth, the first I've seen there; it's the usual awful fluorescent orange – when I was a boy tents were of proper colours, khaki or white or green. I studied the unsuspecting simple-lifers through my bird-watching binoculars – 8.5 x 44 Audubons – they seem to be a fat-bum father, a rangy, muscular mum and a long, lean, grown-up son. I wish them joy of their late holiday, for it has started to rain in a subdued, determined sort of way. Lord Alvanley used to say that his greatest pleasure was to sit in the window of his club and 'watch it rain on the damned people'.

I am simmering a tin of frankfurter sausages on my little butane stove. I have some sliced plastic bread to clothe them in but I wish I had thought to bring mustard and bottled beer. Still, appetite and fresh air make a fine relish: I shall eat like a Boy Scout. 'Palate, the hutch of tasty lust, Desire not to be rinsed with wine.'

The same day, I think

I have been very abstemious with the whisky: I still have one and a quarter bottles of the lovely bully; when these are gone I shall have to sally forth and restock. Food is running short: I have two large cans of beans, one ditto of corned beef, a third of a sliced loaf and five rashers of bacon. (I must eat those raw: the smell of frying bacon carries for miles, did you know?) The local magnates, I fear, are going to lose a pheasant or two in the near future; they are still quite tame for they have not been shot at yet. The pheasants, I mean, not the magnates. I dread the thought of plucking and dressing them – again I mean the pheasants – I used not to mind but my stomach is more tremulous nowadays. Perhaps I shall simply emulate Nebuchadnezzar, that princely poephage, and *graze*. (Now, here's the *good* news: there's plenty of it.)

Is feels like Tuesday, but I could be wrong

After my icy morning wash I have climbed circuitously to the highest point of the Crag, marked FORT on the map. Far below me I can see the gamekeeper's Landrover bouncing and splashing along the half-flooded causeway towards his release pens on the near side of the Moss, and the RSPB warden pottering about usefully in a boat on the Scrape. People often marvel at the existence of a successful bird sanctuary in a shooting preserve but there is no real paradox: what better place for a shy bird to breed than a well-keepered shoot? Shooting only takes place long after the breeding season, after all, and serious sportsmen – nearly all good naturalists – would no more shoots rare bird than their own wives. All right, perhaps they do sometimes shoot a rarity by accident, but then we sometimes shoot our own wives, on purpose, don't we?

I am looking on this skulking period as a kind of holiday and I'm sure it's doing me a power of good. With any luck my ill-wishers are miles away, combing the Lake District for me and terrorizing the campers there. Indeed, they may have decided that I died with Jock; they may all have gone home. If I only had a few bottles of beer I would be feeling positively serene.

Noon

I have been *lulling* myself again.

I made my usual binocular survey ten minutes ago, before venturing forth to the little deserted vertical shaft which I have been using as a lavatory. The Fleagarth tent was apparently deserted, probably, I thought, they were all inside playing cosy games. (Incest – The Game That All the Family Enjoys?) I had crept to within thirty yards of the natural latrine before I smelled the sweet, chocolatey smell of American pipe tobacco. Parting the brambles I saw, standing with his back to me, the form of a long, lean young man, apparently using *my* privy. He was not in fact using it; just looking. He went on looking. He had an American haircut and wore those unbecoming Bermuda shorts. I didn't wait for him to turn around – I never could tell one young American from another – I just eased gently backwards and stole silently back here to my paint mine.

I am sure he is one of the Fleagarth campers: what can he have been doing? Perhaps he is a geologist, perhaps an inefficient badger-watcher, perhaps just an idiot; but the deep, sickening sensation in my belly will not be assuaged by these hypotheses. My belly is convinced that Fleagarth holds an anti-Mortdecai squad. Idle to wonder which lot they are – I can think of very few people who are not anti-Mortdecai this week.

Latter

> 'Finish, good lady, the bright day is done
> And we are for the dark.'

This is it, or that is that; slice it where you will, the game's up. For several minutes just now I had the whole Fleagarth Mob in my field-glasses through a gap in the bramble defences. The thin American – whose shoulders are broader every time I study him – is perhaps one of the Smith and Jones comedy act I met in the sheriff's office in New Mexico; perhaps he is Colonel Blucher; it doesn't matter, probably their own mummies couldn't tell them apart. The burly female part of the sketch I seem to know, I fancy I last saw her fuming in a Triumph Herald at Piccadilly Circus, *you* remember. From the way she handles herself I'd say she was past child bearing but not past entering Judoka contests at Black Belt level.

Grow old along with me – if you're quick – if you're quick – for the best is yet to be. The *tertium quid,* the fat-bummed daddy-figure is – oh, you've guessed it – yes; Martland. Excepting myself, I've never seen anyone more ripe for death. Why I should hate him so much I cannot understand, he has never done me any serious harm; yet.

My recce this afternoon didn't get very far; before I parted my *porte-cochère* of bramble I heard the sound of water buffaloes tramping through a swamp: it was Martland himself, on all fours, being a Woodcraft Indian, looking for *spoor.* Back I slunk, mustering a faint giggle. I could have shot him there and then, I nearly did. I could scarcely have missed the pungent, powdered division of his suety nates as he bent over – he's going to get it in the end, why not that end? Take, oh take those hips away, that so sweetly were forsworn at Hailsham College for the Sons of Officers, and elsewhere.

But I am saving powder and shot for when – if – they find my creep-hole; this Smith and Wesson discharged in a narrow mine-shaft will sound enough like a poacher's twelve-bore to bring the keeper and his two-fisted mates running: I wouldn't give anything for Martland & Co's chances against a determined keeper at this time of the year. Poor Martland, he hasn't tackled anything rougher than a traffic warden since the War.

They are all supping cocoa or something around a wet and smokey woodfire outside their tent in Fleagarth: I have studied them carefully through the glasses and there is positively no deception.

What, still alive at forty-two – a fine upstanding chap like you?

Well, yes.
     Just.
     My manuscript, interlarded with useful currency notes, lies in the bowels of a Winston pillar box, en route for La Maison Spon. I wonder whose eyes will read these last jottings, whose scissors trim away which indiscretions, whose hand strike the match to burn them? Perhaps only your eyes, Blucher. Not yours, I hope, Martland, for I intend that you shall accompany me down to wherever naughty art dealers go when they die. And I shall not let you hold my hand.

They were all out on the Crag in the dark when I returned from Warton; it was a nightmare. For them too, I imagine. I have only a confused memory of creeping and quaking, stalking and counter-stalking, straining aching ears into the blackness and hearing more sounds than there were; finally, the mindless panic of knowing that I was lost.

I regrouped my mental forces – sadly depleted – and forced myself to crouch in a hole until I could orient myself and calm the jam session of my nerves. I had almost succeeded in becoming Major the

Honble Dashwood 'Mad Jack' Mortdecai, V.D. and Scar, the ice-cool toast of the Ypres Salient, when a voice close beside me said, 'Charlie?'

I vomited up my heart, bit it savagely and swallowed it again. My eyes were shut fast, waiting for the shot.

'No,' came a whisper from behind me, 'it's me.' My heart shook itself, tried a tentative beat or two, settled into some sort of ragged rhythm. Martland and the woman rustled about a bit then floundered quietly down the slope.

Where was the American? He was at my lavatory again, that's where he was. Probably booby-trapping it. I think he heard me coming, for all movement stopped. I lowered myself to the ground with infinite caution and could see him, eight feet tall against the sky. He took a noiseless step toward me, then another. To my surprise I was now quite calm, the wanky old avenger preparing to kill his man. My pistol was in the paint mine – just as well, perhaps. First, kick in the family jewels, I decided; second, leg-sweep behind knees; third, bounce rock on head until tender. If no rock, drop knee on face, break hyoid bone in throat with side of hand. Should serve. I began positively to look forward to his next step, although I am not a violent man by nature.

He took the next step – a cock pheasant exploded from under his feet with all the racket and drama of, well, of a rocketing cock pheasant. Now, one of the few things which do not startle old country-bred Mortdecai is a rocketing pheasant, but it was not so with the American; he squeaked, jumped, ducked, crouched and dragged out a great long thing which can only have been an automatic with a silencer fitted. As the shards of silence reassembled themselves I could hear him panting painfully in the dark. At last he rose, tucked the pistol away and drifted off down the slope, thoroughly ashamed of himself, I hope.

I had to come back here to the mine; pistol, food, suitcase and bicycle were and are all here: I need them all except, perhaps, the bicycle.

There is a safe and smelly smugness about this little grave already: I can scarcely hope that they will not nose me out but they cannot, after all, put me further underground than this. There's a Stalingrad for all of us somewhere

> 'Ici gît qui, pour avoir trop aimer les gaupes,
> Desceadit, jeune encore, au royaume des taupes.'

In any case, to run now would be to die sooner, in some spot of their choosing and in some way I might not much like. I prefer it here, where I dreamed the dreams of youth and, later, lifted many a lawless leg – to use the words of R. Burns (1759-96).

You will not find it hard to believe that, since returning to this, my oubliette, I have had more than one suck at my brother's delicious whisky. I intend to have a couple more, then to consult sagacious sleep.

Only a little later

Why we so used to relish the life stories of condemned men, and why so many of us mourn the passing of capital punishment, is because ordinary decent chaps like us have a fine feeling for the dramatic pro-prieties: we know that tragedy cannot properly end in nine years' comfy incarceration and useful, satisfying work in the prison bakery. We know that death is the only end of art. A chap who has gone to all the trouble of strangling his wife is *entitled* to his moment of splen-dour on the gallows – it is a crime to make him sew mailbags like a common thief.

We loved those tales told at the gallows-foot because they freed us from the tyranny and vulgarity of the happy ending; the long, idiot senescence, the wonderful grandchildren, the tactful inquiries about the life-insurance premiums.

Positively the last day – booking for smoking-concerts now

Since there's no help, come then, let's kiss and part. Something has gone wrong. I shall attract no help by firing my pistol, for today is evidently the first of September: duck shooting has begun and since before dawn the Moss and the shore have echoed with sporting musketry.

Martland has found me; I suppose I always knew he would. He came to the mouth of the mine and called down to me. I didn't answer.

'Charlie, we know you're down there, we can *smell you,* for God's sake! Look, Charlie, the others can't hear me, I'm willing to give you a break. Tell me where the bloody picture is, get me off the hook, and I'll give you a night's start; you might get clear away.'

He *can't* have thought I'd believe that, can he?

'Charlie, we've got Jock, he's alive . . .'

I knew that was a lie and suddenly I was filled with rage at his shabbiness. Without exposing myself I aimed the .455 at a knob of rock near the entrance and loosed off around. The noise deafened me momentarily but I could still hear the snarl of the big distorted bullet ricocheting toward Martland. When he spoke again, from another spot, his voice was tight with fear and hatred.

'All right, Mortdecai. Here's another deal. Tell me where the bloody picture is and where the other photographs are and I promise I'll shoot you cleanly. That's the most you can hope for now – and you'll have to trust me even for that.' He enjoyed that bit. I fired again, praying that the mangled lead would take his face off. He spoke again, explaining how void my chances were, not understanding that I had written off my life and wanted only his. He listed lovingly the people who wanted me dead, from the Spanish Government to the Lord's Day Observance Society – I was positively flattered at the extent of the mess I had made. Then he went away.

Later they shot at me with a silenced pistol for half an hour, listening between shots for a cry of pain or surrender. The slugs, screaming and buzzing as they tore from wall to wall, nearly drove me insane but only one touched me; they didn't know whether the shaft turned left or right. The one lucky shot laid my scalp open and it is bleeding into my eyes – I must look a *sight*.

The American tried coaxing me next but he, too, had nothing to offer but a quick death in exchange for information and a written confession. They must have raised the Rolls from its grave in the canyon, for he knows the Goya wasn't in the soft-top. Spain, it seems, is due to renew a treaty with the USA about Strategic Air Force bases on her territory, but every time the US reminds them about it, the Spaniards change the subject to the Goya. 'Duchess of Wellington' – 'known to have been stolen on behalf of an American and to have entered the US.' He wouldn't have told me about the bases if he thought I had any chance of surviving, would he?

I didn't bother to reply, I was busy with the turpentine.

Then he told me the alternative, the *dirty* death: they have sent for a canister of cyanide, the stuff they use on rabbits here and on people over there. So evidently I cannot hope for Martland to come down and fetch me. I shall have to go out to him. It's of no importance.

I have finished with the turpentine; mixed with whisky it has served beautifully to dissolve the lining of my suitcase and now the Goya smiles at me from the wall, fresh and lovely as the day she was painted, the incomparable, naked 'Duquesa de Wellington,' mine to keep for the rest of my life. *'Donc, Dieu existe.'*

There is enough whisky to last me until the light fades and then – who could be afraid? – I shall emerge with my six-gun blazing, like some shaggy hero of the Old West. I know that I shall be able to kill Martland; then one of the others will kill me and I shall fall like a bright exhalation in the evening down to hell where there is no art and no alcohol, for this is, after all, quite a moral tale. You see that, don't you?